WACS AT WORK

By FJERIL HESS

WACS AT WORK

The Story of the "Three B's" of the AAF

By FJERIL HESS

THE MACMILLAN COMPANY · NEW YORK

1945

TO

THE ENLISTED WOMEN

OF THE WOMEN'S ARMY CORPS

AND ESPECIALLY FOR

SERGEANT JAN SHEETS

AND

CORPORAL L. MARJORIE SEARLES

CONTENTS

CHAPTER I

"Spring Came On Forever"

"They spoke, I think, of perils past.
They spoke, I think, of peace at last.
One thing I remember:
Spring came on forever.
Spring came on forever,
Said the Chinese nightingale."

Pete spoke the words drowsily into the silence that had fallen on the group of five friends stretched out at ease on the grass. The warmth of the early Southern spring was tempered by the thick growth of dark green pines that surrounded the small clearing near the barracks, relaxing and welcome after the excitement of what had turned out to be a very special last day of WAAC basic training at Fort Oglethorpe, Georgia.

"Our Post Poet," said Sue Bates, rolling over on her side to rumple Pete's short brown curls. She flicked a daddy-long-legs from her friend's shoulder and smiled lazily at their civilian visitor, Ann Dudley, who sat looking down at the four khaki-clad forms grouped around her. "She even writes the stuff," she added with pretended scorn, and tickled Pete's ear with a pine needle.

A groan came from the chubby figure lying face down on the grass as the round brown head burrowed still deeper into outstretched arms.

1

"I met Vachel Lindsay once, long before he had written 'The Chinese Nightingale.'" Ann looked off into the distance and counted rapidly on her fingers. "Good heavens, that must have been before any of you children were born."

Pete smiled lazily at Ann; then she made a face at Sue as she hunched closer to this new friend who had come to Fort Oglethorpe at the invitation of Sue Bates and Angela Borelli, both of whom she had known before they enlisted in the Women's Army Auxiliary Corps.*

"It would take a poet, and a good one, to do justice to the sight of you all sweeping across the parade ground today, with your own WAAC band playing and the company guidons held out by the breeze. I could pick out Josephine and was bursting with pride, for I thought she was the finest guidon bearer of them all. It made me feel very proprietary, Jo, in spite of having known you only a few hours."

Jo Barrows flexed her right wrist and pumped her arm up and down with a reminiscent smile.

"I was scared silly that I'd make a bungle of it, today of all days. It's awfully easy to miss your armpit when you lower the staff. I gave a heave of relief when we had passed the reviewing stand. The staff seems plenty long when you're carrying it against your shoulder. Then, when you whip it down for the salute, you have a sickening feeling that you'll either drop the darn thing or swing it outside your elbow."

"I consider myself an especially privileged guest to have been here for the great occasion. I'll wager it was one of the most thrilling graduation days any company has had. Did you have any idea it was going to be so special when you asked me over?"

---

* The WAAC did not become a part of the regular Army until August, 1943.

Stewart Field (N. Y.) WAC's salute during the impressive retreat
ceremony held each day.

Both Angela and Sue sat up eagerly to answer Ann's question; then Sue dropped back on the grass and waved her hands helplessly.

"You tell it, Angel. I'm still weak from that wonderful review we put on. Boy! Were we good!"

Angela smiled at Sue's enthusiasm, but her own eyes reflected her outspoken satisfaction.

"Usually there is no special celebration when a company finishes basic training. No special graduation ceremonies, I mean. A big company party, of course, is put on before the final day, with an entertainment of some kind. That's a big occasion and is looked forward to all through training. Today, however, we were blown out first thing and told to clean the barracks and the grounds with a toothbrush, if necessary. And what an inspection we had! We felt mighty good when the company commander complimented us on it.

"Then we were told to get into visor caps, gloves, and complete khaki uniforms and to see to it that our shoes were mirrors. By that time everybody knew something special was in the wind and rumors began to fly around that some important person was at the Fort, or going to be."

"But even the rumors weren't wild enough to hint at who that person was."

Sue couldn't keep quiet any longer, so she propped herself up on one elbow to continue the account.

"We were 'hutted' to the parade ground, where we saw the garrison flag was flying. Then we *knew* something was going to happen, because only a very important somebody or occasion rates the garrison flag."

Seeing a question in Ann's eyes, Jo interrupted Sue's hurrying words.

"We didn't know what a garrison flag was, either, until a few short weeks ago," she explained. "There are four dif-

4

ferent names for the Flag of the United States in military service: flag, color, standard, and ensign."

Jo counted them off soberly on her fingers.

"A *color* is a flag carried by dismounted units and so forth. A *standard* is a flag carried by mounted or motorized units. An *ensign* is a flag flown on ships, small boats, and airships. But when we say flag, ordinarily, we don't mean any of those. Does this bore you?" she asked Ann suddenly.

"No, indeed. Haven't I been popping questions at you all day? It makes me feel terrifically civilian not to know the difference between a garrison flag and a regular flag, but there you are. Go on, Jo, and educate me."

In the back of her mind as she listened, Ann found herself wondering, as she had so many times during the past few hours, what effect this new life was going to have on these girls who had fallen into Army ways with such apparent ease. In spite of her interest in all their activities she was concerned somewhat about what would happen to them when the war was over. She was still inclined to think that the regimentation of Army life was a strange kind of education for young citizens of a democracy. She knew she would have much food for thought after this visit. Meanwhile their enthusiasm for their Corps, and their pride in their new experience and what they hoped to accomplish, was contagious and she found that she was genuinely interested in knowing about the sizes of flags and the ceremonies connected with them.

When Jo had finished her explanation Ann proved that she had listened carefully by reviewing the facts, to Sue's great amusement.

"I ought to be able to remember that a garrison flag is twice as large as a post flag and a storm flag is half as large as a post flag. Now if I can just keep in mind that the garrison flag is thirty-eight feet by twenty feet and displayed only on important occasions, I ought to be able to work down to the nine feet six inches by five feet stormy or windy weather flag."

"Good for you," crowed Sue. "I never used to be able to remember figures, but I find I can if I put my mind to it. Now that we have flag dimensions under control, thanks to Josie, there was the garrison flag looking like a million dollars when we reached the parade ground. The breeze lifted it up against the sky and the sight of it helped to buck us up while we stood around for what seemed like hours.

"Finally the bugle call brought us to attention and, though we could see nothing as yet, we stood at attention for about five more minutes. You know what happened next, for you had arrived by that time with your friends from Chattanooga."

"I certainly do know. I saw you all out there on the big green field at attention and my spine began to prickle even before the cannon at the far end of the field began to boom."

"I held my breath during all of those twenty-one rounds," said Pete, sitting bolt upright and running her hands through her hair until her curls stood out from her head in spirals. "I can still feel the chills that ran up and down my back, because they told us that the visitor was the Commander in Chief himself. When all you civilians at the far side of the parade ground set up a wild cheer, I had to bite the inside of my cheek to keep my own hoorays down.

"But there we were, at attention, and could only listen and shiver. When the crowd quieted down and the parade began I wondered if my legs would hold me up."

"I guess we all did," said Angela quietly. "But we marched as if inspired. You could just feel an electric current pass from line to line, and for once I think we were letter-perfect. At least Colonel Brown, the Commandant of the Post, said he didn't see a single person out of step or a single one who was not marching at attention. And that, Ann, is practically a miracle."

"It was truly a miracle to watch," agreed Ann enthusiastically. "When I heard the command 'Eyes right,' and every head and every pair of eyes snapped at the same time, I had to dig my nails into the palms of my hands to keep the tears back. I stood where I could see the President and I felt that he was tremendously moved."

"Could you see his little dog, Fala, too?" asked Pete. "His black face looked so darned cute resting on his forefeet, which hung over the side of the open car, that I would have had a hard time to keep a grin off my face if my muscles hadn't been as frozen as Birdseye peas. He looked for all the world as if he were standing the review, too. I'll never forget this day if I live to be a hundred. You can just imagine how it felt to be actually passing in review for the Commander in Chief of the United States Army. Whew!"

Pete threw herself back on the ground, relaxing again from the tenseness of reliving for a few moments the strain and excitement of that review.

"I know what it was like to watch you," said Ann, smiling at Angela. "I shan't forget it, either—ever. It was so much more than a ceremonial beautifully executed. In fact, I find myself quite at a loss for words with which to describe its effect on me—and my business is words, you know."

"We know what you mean," said Angela gravely. "Your heart has to be in your beliefs as well as your mind. It's like the flags Jo was telling you about. Your mind knows that a garrison flag is one size and a post flag another; but it's your heart that puts meaning into the Stars and Stripes, whatever size they may be. I think my father made me see that, long before I ever thought of going into the WAAC. I'll never forget how proud he was when he held his citizen-

7

ship papers in his hands and told us children how he felt about being a real honest-to-goodness citizen of the United States. Somehow it made us all feel more like citizens, too, even though we had all been born over here."

For a while the talk was an eager exchange concerning persons and incidents unfamiliar to Ann, so she studied the girls before her on the ground.

Sue and Angela, she decided, had both benefited in their own individual ways by their weeks of basic training. Angela had been an assistant in the production department of the publishing house in New York where Ann worked, and Sue had been her secretary for over two years. Angela, who was twenty-two and had earned her own living for several years, had grown more sure of herself, more decisive, while Sue, a year younger but much more sophisticated in outer manner at least, had become a trifle more subdued and decidedly more mannerly. Ann had been fond of them both and, since a brief vacation with friends in Chattanooga had coincided with the end of their training at Fort Oglethorpe, she had gladly accepted their urgent invitation to visit them on this last day of their training.

Her own busy office, with her desk piled high with problems dealing with printed words, seemed very remote among the thousands of girls and women who were in one stage or another of training at this sprawling, long-established military post.

Josephine Barrows, Ann mused, was the most independent member of the group and a natural leader. She was tall and slender, with such poise and naturalness of manner that she seemed older than the other girls, though Ann knew that both she and Pete had passed their twentieth birthdays just before joining the WAAC. Her uniform suited her honey-colored hair and golden skin perfectly, and, though she was stretched at ease on the ground, she did not lounge.

She and Angela hadn't a sprawl in their make-up, Ann thought; but Jo's composure seemed a part of her nature, while to Angela it was a rule of conduct.

Dorothy Peterson, whom everyone on the post called Pete, was full of surprises, apparently, and many contrasts. Ann could hardly recognize in this dreamy-eyed quoter of verses the high-spirited, effervescent girl who had been the ringleader in showing off the Fort to the visitor from New York. Ann had been ready to drop with fatigue when Pete had suddenly proposed a trip to the clearing, which was a favorite meeting place, in good weather, of the four friends. Once arrived in this secluded spot, she had been the most relaxed and quiet of the four graduates.

As Ann's eyes rested speculatively on Pete's motionless form, she heard a quiet chuckle and turned to find Jo's brown eyes fixed curiously on her.

"Now that you've sized up all of us, be a sport and give us a character reading—a sort of forecast about what you think will happen to us in this man's army."

Amused that she had been caught in the act of doing just what Josephine accused her of, Ann protested that her wits had been woolgathering.

"I don't know enough about you and Dorothy to make any prognostications."

"Our boss!" said Sue, leaning over to nudge Angela. "Still uses those sixty-dollar words. Even without any crystal ball I'll predict that our Josie will be on her way to Officer Candidate School, and within a few short weeks will be promoted to company commander, and end up overseas as head of a battalion or something. After all, Jo, you're the only college graduate in our gang. Besides, Lieutenant Bill Garland made a date with you to meet him in North Africa. Remember?"

Instead of answering Sue's banter in the same spirit,

9

Josephine twisted the engagement ring on her finger. She picked up a handful of dry pine needles and, crushing them in her hands, sifted them slowly from one palm to the other.

"Bill has his job of flying to do and I'll have one soon, I hope, though mine will be with both feet on the ground. I haven't any desire to try for OCS. I don't want an administrative job in this business. I want a hard, working-with-my-hands kind of job—something that I can see and feel and get dirty doing, if necessary. And I have no desire to go overseas, strangely enough. I want to stay right here and do all I can to help bring our men back home just as fast as we can bring them."

"We all want to do that."

Angela spoke quietly, but her blue eyes seemed to take on deeper color as they looked earnestly into Ann's.

"There are lots of times, of course, when it seems to us as if the officers had the best of it, but we don't forget that the enlisted man or woman is the heart of the Army. And what good is a head without any heart? I want terribly to go overseas—to Italy, perhaps—when the time comes, but if I can't go I'm very willing to do whatever job is given me to do. I speak Italian, of course, and I know it would give my father a big thrill if I were sent to Italy. Both my brothers are in the Army, you know, but one is in the South Pacific and the other in Alaska. As for being an officer, I think I feel as Jo does. I like to work with my hands, you know."

"Just the same, I'll be waiting expectantly to hear about your first stripe. You wouldn't object to having a few of those, would you?"

"They don't come easy, ma'am." Pete patted the upper part of her sleeves tenderly. "Boy! When I can run my fingers over my arms and feel a little ridge under 'em, I'm going to be prouder than any old second looey is of her

10

gold bars. Why don't you join the Corps, ma'am?" she asked abruptly, turning impulsively toward Ann. "We need women like you and you'd love it, just as we do. It's the best thing I ever did and I'll never forget the moment when I was sworn in and said 'I do.' Even that review today didn't get me any harder by the throat.

"And what the Army has done for one Dorothy Peterson, you just wouldn't believe. Why, I'm getting so I couldn't be late or untidy or slap-happy any more—even without gigs and regulations."

She sat up and began to comb bits of grass and pine needles from her hair with vigorous fingers. She looked keenly at Ann Dudley's poised figure; at her slim strong hands, her well-tailored gray suit and dainty blouse; at her dark, neat curling hair with its touch of gray at the temples; and, last, at the trim ankles and high-heeled pumps.

"You might have a hard time getting used to gruesome twosomes," she said finally, inspecting her own sturdy brown shoes, "but I bet you'd look swell in one of those new super-dooper tropical worsteds like the CO's. Me, I'm strictly GI and glad of it."

"Sour grapes," scoffed Sue, bending over to brush the ants from Angela's back. "Pallas Athena's daughter has ants in her toga, Angel. And in her helmet too."

She flipped the shining new disk fastened to the front of the visored hat, to free it of the invaders, and gazed at the spread eagle thoughtfully.

Angela Borelli, small and dark, whose every movement was graceful, took her hat from Sue's hands and set it firmly on her head, allowing only a glimpse of her straight black hair that was gathered in a close smooth knot above her collar. The effect was quite beautiful, Ann noted, though such severity of line in both hat and hair would have been trying to a face less lovely than Angela's. Her intensely

11

blue eyes—northern Italian eyes—had a twinkle in them as they met Ann's, and her husky pleasant voice had none of Sue's bluster when she spoke.

"The toga was worn by Roman citizens, Susie, and our goddess was Greek. A gig for that, my friend. Now ants in the armor would be something else again."

"You're telling me!" moaned Pete, opening her collar with a great jingle of dog tags to search for an unwelcome visitor. "Darn this hardware anyhow. I've taken to sleeping in mine ever since about half the company was put on special duty for going without them."

"How would anyone discover you didn't have them around your neck? They don't show," said Ann, looking at the metal tags that gave the wearer's name, rank, serial number, blood type, and so on.

"They stop you and demand to see them," giggled Pete. "That's how. Mine show most of the time anyway. Every time I bend over, out they pop no matter how tightly I tuck them in. All of a sudden the MPs or the officers break out in a rash of wanting to see dog tags and it's always on the day that everybody decided they just couldn't stand to go around jingling any longer."

"If the Corps is taken into the Army, will you still wear the head of Pallas Athena?"

Ann studied the head of the Greek goddess on the collar insigne of the girls' uniforms as she spoke.

"I'm not sure, but rumor has it that we'll wear the insigne of whatever branch of the service we serve with. I only hope I can wear the wings and propeller of the Air Forces one of these days, not that I don't reverence Pallas," added Jo quickly.

She gave Pete's wide expanse of khaki skirt a smart spank and pretended to polish the insigne on her collar with the palm of her hand.

12

"She was almost as busy as a modern WAAC, as I recall. She was also the patroness of agriculture and invented the rake and other implements," Ann said.

"After that session of policing the grounds around the barracks this morning, we could use the rake as an emblem," said Sue, with a deep sigh. "I bet we didn't miss a blade of grass or a single pebble."

"I wish she'd invented a special weed puller to get in under the barracks with. It took three men and a boy to pull me out, once I wiggled into that little bitty space after a few puny little spears that nobody could ever see under there anyhow. I bet no woman ever thought that one up. It's pure useless activity."

"She thought up the olive tree, though, and the gods decreed it was so much more useful than the horse that Poseidon created that they awarded a great city to her, and it was called Athens."

"Speaking of olives, I hope it isn't too long before chow. I'm ravishing."

"Famishing," corrected Jo automatically.

"Ravishing sounds hungrier," Pete insisted.

"And it's more than time for me to be hustling back to Chattanooga if I'm going to make my train back to New York tonight," said Ann as the girls reluctantly arose and began brushing off their uniforms. "Goodness knows when I'll see you two infants again."

Ann put her arms around Sue and Angela and included Pete and Josephine in a warm smile for all four girls.

"It has been a wonderful experience for a mere civilian to have a small share in this big day of yours. I'll be very eager to hear from all of you when you've settled into your new duties. I wish I knew where you are going to be, but no doubt you'll scatter to the four winds. Except Dorothy. I know she is to stay here at the Fort."

13

"Please call me Pete, ma'am. After all, you're a member of the gang now—representing all of our fond families, as you have."

"If you won't call me ma'am, I will. And everybody finds it easy to call me Ann, you know."

Pete blushed and looked so respectful that Ann felt twice her forty years even while she had to laugh.

"I even call my Mom 'ma'am' now and the poor darling nearly has heart failure every time I do. It gets to be a habit, you know, when you say it to your officers five hundred times a day.

"Just look at my skirt, and after I stood up all morning, too, so it wouldn't have a wrinkle in it. That's the trouble with these darned 'sun tans' of ours. I don't know why it is that Angel and Jo can look like something out of *Vogue* long after Susie and I begin to resemble very dried apricots."

"We've learned how to lean on things to take the weight off our feet," explained Jo, a trifle airily.

"From now on 'things' will be leaning on me," chuckled Pete, working at her stockings so that the seams ran straight up the back of her sturdy legs. "When I remember how green I was a few weeks ago, I get a kick out of being an old-timer around the place. Something like the way we used to feel when we were kids in our second or third year at Girl Scout camp: very, very superior—and responsible, of course —to the little greenhorns sleeping out in the big woods for the first time in their lives."

"She's still a Girl Scout at heart," teased Sue.

Pete shrugged and grinned good-naturedly.

"Sure I am, and proud of it. You just ought to see the letters the kids who used to be in my troop write to me. Gee whiz, they're proud of their old leader for being one of Uncle Sam's girls. I've been taken on many a hay ride for it, too, ma'am. But what's so sissy about trying to teach kids to

14

learn to take care of themselves and wanting to be of service in this poor old cockeyed world? Why, you'd be amazed at the number of officers and cadre who don't even know how to build a simple fire, for instance. When anybody gives me the old sneer about sissy-prissy Scouts, I give 'em what for—right back. It works too, eventually, but I've taken plenty."

"I was only teasing," said Sue apologetically.

"I know you were and I didn't mean to get on a soapbox either. We get the same kind of ribbing for being WAACs sometimes, but there's no use getting belligerent about it. All you can do is make sure that you're a darn good member of the Corps and get on with the job."

"Bravo!" said Ann. "I'll remember that, Pete. And if I catch myself falling into bad habits, I'll give myself ten demerits—or gigs as you call them. A civilian has a lot of new words to learn, you see. What does cadre mean?"

Somewhat flushed by her impetuous outburst, Pete launched into such a lengthy explanation of company organization that Jo realized Ann was completely at sea. She interrupted the spate of words tactfully but effectually, to Ann's secret amusement.

"Cadre is a French word meaning nucleus. As rookies come in for training, a cadre of about three to six noncoms helps to build up a company and takes charge of the needs of the group."

"And what happens next to the Three B's—Barrows, Bates, and Borelli?"

"I'm afraid we'll be only Two B's from now on. Sue and I go to Kansas City for specialized radio training for about three months, and Angel doesn't know yet where she'll be sent. We were hoping all four of us could stay together, but that's just too much to expect."

"You have no idea, I suppose, where you will be sent eventually?"

15

"Not the remotest, ma'am. I've got the ma'ams, too, you see. We've learned that what you *think* is going to happen in the Army seldom does! We hope we'll end up with the Air Forces somewhere, but that's probably just one of those dreams. When we finish our radio training, we'll be sent to a staging area to become part of a new company and be shipped out for a more or less permanent assignment, I suppose."

"Permanent!" scoffed Pete. "There's no such word for our generation."

"Nonsense, and you with your 'spring came on forevers'! We wouldn't be here, any of the four of us, if we didn't believe in some permanencies."

Sue stuttered slightly over the last word, but she sounded so serious that no one laughed at her unexpected outburst. She looked at Ann and smiled a trifle self-consciously before continuing.

"I know what Pete meant all right, and I'll admit I didn't enlist because of any high-flown motives. I wanted to be in the swim, I suppose, as much as anything. Being a WAAC seemed a good definite idea. After all, I'm a literal-minded person. That's why I didn't mind the grind of basic as much as Angela and Jo, for instance. But, darn it, I got more out of it than 'Hut-two-three-four' and I'd say I'm just about a good average example."

Long after Ann Dudley had left the Fort that afternoon the faces of the four girls remained vivid in her memory. In spite of the great differences in their personal background, education, and experience they had undoubtedly found common grounds that were strong enough to support a sound friendship.

She gazed out of the window as her train carried her swiftly northward. The accumulation of work awaiting her no longer depressed her, remembering many of the real sacrifices that thousands of girls like Jo and Pete and her own two special friends, Sue and Angela, had made in the service of their country, different as their motives might have been.

The few hours she had spent with them at Fort Oglethorpe had given far more refreshment to her work-weary nerves, and more stimulation to her imagination, than the lazy pleasant hours of her short holiday spent with easygoing friends of her own age.

She was aware, nevertheless, of a new restlessness, almost dissatisfaction, at having to take what seemed a passive role in the war effort in contrast to the work that younger women were engaging in so eagerly.

"Ann Dudley—just old civilian fuddy-duddy," she fumed, and was startled by feeling almost resentful over facing the regular routine of business and the rather humdrum volunteer work that she did several evenings a week.

"It was that plagued band and the flags against the blue sky and youth with its face lifted to the sun, you old fool," she scolded herself, when the mood showed no signs of wearing off.

She gave herself a little shake and looked down at her trim pumps, which had a decidedly scuffed appearance after their travels over parade ground and woods' paths.

"Gruesome twosomes!" she thought ruefully, remembering the term Pete had applied to her own stout brown oxfords.

She closed her eyes and could see again the sweep and beauty of marching women. As thrilling as that demonstration of unity and coordination had been, it was the spirit and purpose back of the perfection of movement that had moved her so strongly.

"And mind you keep in cadence," she warned; but, while her eyes were upon the scratched toes of her shoes, her admonishment was for inner consumption.

17

CHAPTER II

In on the Beam

" 'Adam and Eve and Pinch Me went down to the river to swim,' " quoted Jo in a low voice to Sue and Angela as their close-curtained GI truck rolled along the highway on the last lap of their long journey to the post to which they had been assigned.

Angela looked puzzled when Sue giggled and finished the childish riddle.

" 'Adam and Eve were drowned and who was saved? Pinch Me.' My gosh, I haven't thought of that old thing since I was a kid."

"I never heard it before," confessed Angela, "but I wish someone would nip me to make me realize this is real and that we three are actually on our way to an air base. Remember how we used to say that miracles don't happen in the Army?"

"It's too bad Pete isn't along too. But I guess even the Air Forces couldn't tempt her away from her old chemical-warfare stuff. Ugh! She can have it. I nearly died every time I had to put on my gas mask during basic, let alone go through the gas chamber. I hope we're finished with that kind of business now."

Sue shrugged with distaste, but she was wedged so tightly between her neighbors in the close-packed truck that she aroused a protest.

18

The reunion of the Three B's, as Ann Dudley had called them, at the staging area to which Sue and Jo had been sent upon completing their three months' course at the radio school in Kansas, had increased the anticipation with which they looked forward to being assigned to actual jobs. During those three months Angela had felt she was more or less marking time on a temporary assignment, so she was as thrilled as the other two girls to be a member of the first WAAC detachment assigned to the base for which they were now heading.

"It's a dark night and smells of cheese," continued Jo as the truck rumbled along at a steady pace.

"Wish I had some cheese—about half a pound of it— tucked between two nice slabs of bread and butter. You're crazy. I don't smell any, and it's not dark yet."

Sue tried to extract her handkerchief, but she couldn't move her arms enough to get her hand into her shoulder bag.

"Just an old saying in my family. You know, the story of the absent-minded professor whose wife asked him to take a look at the weather? He stuck his head into an old cupboard, thinking it was the window, and came back with that pronouncement. At least it's dark enough in this truck and ought to smell of sardines the way we're packed in here. How do you like being a troop movement?"

"I'd rather see than be one, if you insist on making this a quoting party," Sue answered, with a small sniff. "And it probably will be dark by the time we get settled. Bet we won't even get a squint at our new home. I wonder what it's like."

"Mighty handsome and huge, Captain Cramer says. Wonderful barracks for us that used to be officers' quarters, so we'll be two in a room instead of the usual umpty-seven. At least we'll all be under the same roof if we're assigned to quarters alphabetically."

19

Before long the driver slowed his speed to keep at the proper distance from the car ahead and, as soon as the other trucks preceding them had moved on, Jo had a glimpse of the white-helmeted guard at the entrance to the air field and of the high wire fence extending on either side of the entrance gate.

"Looks like a concentration camp," said one of the girls at the back of the truck. "Old Sourpuss at the gate didn't even look at us. We're just so much baggage to him, I suppose."

"What did she expect him to do, throw kisses?" murmured Sue, craning her neck to try to get a glimpse of the parklike area they were entering.

As the trucks wound out of sight with their freight of tired, travel-stained WAACs, Private First Class Johnny Samson turned to his fellow guard at the gate and made a large O with the thumb and finger of his right hand.

"Something new has been added," said Johnny significantly. "Thirty days and a lot of soldiers will be on their way."

"Says you. If there are any grease monkeys or truck drivers or radio repairmen in that bunch I'll eat my gaiters. Reinforcements for the Army Chair Corps, probably. Replacement troops for some of the civilians filing carbon copies and playing iron pianos down at headquarters."

"Aw, nuts." Johnny's gesture was more eloquent than words as he brushed aside his companion's opinion. "Where've you been lately? We've been waiting six months to get a bunch of WAACs down here. I thought it was just a pipe dream until I saw those gals with my own eyes. We've had their area all shined up for days, just ready and waiting for them to move in and take over."

"Take over what? Who wants a bunch of women messing around in the Army anyhow?"

20

One job taken over by WAC's at The Army Air Forces bases is that of supply clerk—keeping records and issuing supplies to AAF personnel. The WAC shown here works in the clothing supply section of a large AAF base and is issuing heavy fleece-lined flying suits. The flyer is trying on wool-lined flying boots.

The husky corporal spat into the gravel to express his disapproval and scowled after the line of trucks disappearing into the distance.

Johnny hooked his thumbs into his white holster belt and grinned at the corporal pityingly as he fixed his eyes on the other's spotlessly white canvas gaiters.

"Hope your teeth are in good shape, pal. Those gaiters are going to make tough chewing. Say, I've got a kid sister in the WAVEs who's an aviation mechanic, first class. And don't you forget she didn't get that rating for sitting around on her fanny making up with the dry ammunition, either."

"Dry what?"

Johnny pushed his helmet back and elaborately pantomimed making up his face, while the corporal looked at him with a slow grin curling the corners of his mouth.

The crunch of footsteps on the graveled walk beyond the gatehouse brought both men suddenly to attention, and when the officer of the day approached a moment later their faces were expressionless.

Suddenly the strong clear notes of the Air Force Song reached the guards on duty at the entrance as the post band, full strength, welcomed the newcomers.

"You tell 'em, fellas," muttered Johnny as he listened, wishing he hadn't had the bad luck to be stuck way out here at the gate.

He would have liked to see the girls' faces when they heard the welcome waiting for them down in front of headquarters. He envied the men who had volunteered to help the detachment settle into their new quarters. Nobody could tell him that the entrance of those curtained trucks through the gates he helped to guard wasn't a good omen for the field.

"I'll make up for this tomorrow," he promised himself, and grinned to see the look of interest that began to dawn

22

in Corporal Bevin's eyes as the music floated back to them from headquarters.

Meanwhile the line of trucks bearing the hundred WAACs and their baggage swung around to the right of a huge circular drive enclosing the post parade ground. The band struck up as the first truck rounded the curve, and kept playing while they drew up in front of base headquarters and the girls descended. While their company commander went through the formalities of reporting to the base commander, the detachment formed into columns of four and swung off at a smart pace to the WAAC area, which lay beyond the far end of the long green field. The band, marching abreast of them down the center of the parade ground while the company kept to the broad curving drive, played a lively military air that made marching a double pleasure after the long hours of inactivity on trains and in trucks.

In the eyes of many of the girls were tears of pride and joy at having been given so royal a welcome—first at the end of their train journey, when they had been met by several officers and a flock of noncoms from the air base, plus newspaper photographers, and now by the post band playing in their own special honor.

At their barracks they were dismissed while the trucks moved up with their luggage, which the girls had to sort and tote indoors before they were free to investigate their area.

In the midst of a mountain of luggage that had been unloaded onto the grass in front of the area headquarters stood First Sergeant O'Connell, answering questions and directing the members of the company to the various barracks as calmly and surely as if she had been on the ground weeks instead of minutes.

"Tell 'em to dump their stuff wherever they find a place that isn't already taken for tonight," she advised Jo, who had been giving her a hand. "There's plenty of space—two to a room, for now anyhow. And pass the word around that there'll be coffee and sandwiches in the mess hall for anybody who wants food—as who doesn't! Supply office is down there to the left of the orderly room, so they better start queuing up for blankets and stuff before they go to chow."

"That's what I call human kindness to dumb animals," said Sue fervently, appearing just in time to hear the welcome announcement about food. "I knew our cooks and bakers were good, but I didn't know they were that good. Why, they just got here!"

"And they're already over in the mess hall with their sleeves rolled up, so corral some of those pernickety house hunters and carry their luggage indoors for them. They've got their hands full over in the kitchen trying to get up a meal and keep from falling over about twenty-five GI's who have been helping Lieutenant Nolan the last couple of days."

"If Lieutenant Nolan has been on the job, no wonder we're fixed up with all the comforts of home," said Jo a little later as she waited for Sue and Angela to finish their hasty tidying-up process.

"Call them comforts if you like," grumbled Sue, stumbling over unfamiliar ground in the dark as the Three B's made their way from their barracks to the brightly lighted mess hall near by.

"You should have seen our cozy little hotel quarters in Kansas City, Angel. Running water in our room, maid service, real clothes closets. I've almost forgotten how to hang my stuff up in GI fashion. I feel as if I were back in basic, after standing in a queue again to tote off my own load of sheets, blankets, quilt, mattress cover, and pillow

24

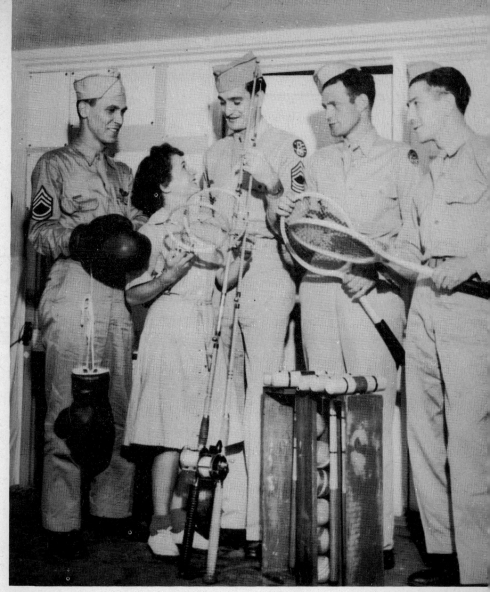

Official U. S. AAF photo

Issuing sports equipment to flyers who have returned to this country after being in combat overseas is the job of this WAC. She works in the sports section of the Special Services Office at the Army Air Forces Redistribution Station No. 1 Atlantic City, N. J. WAC's hold other jobs in Special Services, the office at every army post which has charge of providing entertainment for personnel.

slips. Wow, my arm still aches from lugging them around—and me starving to death."

"It sounds to me as if you'd gotten pretty soft in the last three months. I thought you said you'd never worked so hard in your life as you did at radio school."

"Sue always grumbles when she's hungry. Remember? We worked hard enough to need a little maid service—and loved it, I might add. The work, I mean."

"I'm sure you did or you wouldn't both be wearing corporal's stripes. You're one up on Pete and me—lucky women."

"Luck nothing," said Sue heatedly, stopping dead in the path and buttonholing Angela with a firm hand. "Before we got our little Technician Fifth Grade stripes we had to start with a bag of loose parts and end up with a complete radio set—that worked, mind you. We even had to learn to make pencil strokes all in one direction when transcribing by hand and make exact motions with hands and wrists when handling messages."

Sue demonstrated with quick motions in the gathering darkness, forgetting for a moment that she was on the point of starvation.

"Gosh, Angel, it was a sight to see—two hundred of us in one huge room, men and women, seated at long tables practicing at radio sets or playing around with hack saws, blowtorches, and other tools. I never had so much fun in my life, or learned so much in a short time—me, who three months ago thought a tube was strictly for tooth paste."

"At least you knew how to handle a typewriter," Jo reminded her. "I even had to learn that—and I don't mean Hunt and Peck, either. And the Continental Code! I used to wish I had been a Girl Scout like Pete. Remember how she used to moan because none of us could answer her dots and dashes on the leg of a bed after bed check?"

Official U. S. AAF photo

The dayroom in the WAC area is a busy place when the girls give a party. It is usually the spot where the men come to call for their dates.

"Good old Pete. We'll have to try to get her up here for a visit. And Ann Dudley too. Maybe we could have a real reunion once we get settled down to work."

"Gee whiz, what are we waiting for?" Sue urged when Jo and Angel stopped again and stood looking curiously around them at the cluster of wooden buildings that comprised the WAAC area.

"Are we really here at last?" said Angel softly.

"Yup, this is it."

Jo sounded very matter-of-fact, but her eyes were shining as they turned toward the dim outlines of huge buildings far beyond the units of their own area.

"As Ann said a few weeks ago—or was it a year ago?— it would take a poet to describe how I felt tonight when I heard that band break into the Air Force Song. I had goose pimples on top of goose pimples."

"Me too."

Sue's words ended in a sigh of great content; then her voice bubbled up again as she clutched Angela's arm and held on tight to it.

"Those officers from the base were so friendly and informal when they met us at the train. They even looked surprised when we said 'sir' to them. At least I didn't forget and say 'ma'am.' It's a good thing you met your Bill before you became a WAAC, Josie. Some of those lads had a mighty nice twinkle in their eyes tonight."

Another deep sigh from Sue indicated her regret over the fact that officers were forbidden territory, as far as she was concerned.

A distant hum of motors silenced her in the middle of another ecstatic sentence and the three friends searched the dark sky above the airfield for signs of a plane.

"There he is!" cried Sue, pointing to the south.

They watched the lights of a plane as it curved in over

the field and dropped down out of sight with a roar of sound that became a series of snorts and then silence.

"Sharp eyes, Susie," said Jo admiringly. "We'll have to get you a job in the control tower."

"Oh, my eyes are sharp enough; but so is my tongue, unfortunately. I wish you two would sort of hit me over the head every time I start speaking out of turn. O'Connell would have to walk by just when I was griping about comforts. Hope she didn't hear me. Heck, I'm so darn glad to be on an airfield I don't care what happens from now on. Let's eat."

"Two witnesses, Susie. So watch yourself! Anyhow, happy landings to all of us. We sure came in on the beam tonight, at any rate."

With a last long look at the great revolving light that seemed to be flashing them a special welcome through the darkness, the Three B's stepped across the threshold of their own mess hall feeling that somehow they had already become part of a busy new life.

CHAPTER III

Settling In

After repeated prods from Jo, Sue opened one eye and blinked at her reproachfully.

"Don't tell me—let me guess," she groaned, burying her head in her pillow for one last moment before tearing herself out of bed and groping for her shoes and stockings.

"Reveille, remember, Corporal Bates?"

"Oh, for the good old days when we lived like lords— no KP, no police duty, no PT, no— Gosh, I forgot! No more grumbling."

"That's better. Now step on it. We're going to have fifteen minutes of physical training after roll call, so jump into your fatigues. You've got five minutes, Susie. Don't disgrace the Three B's on our very first morning."

"And don't you go pulling your eyebrows down on me, my fine Technician Fifth Grade, or I'll mow you down."

"Mow the lawn is more likely. Just wait till you see the area by full daylight—grass and flowering shrubs and nice graveled walks all over the place. It would be a pleasure to police these grounds."

"Don't tell me you've been up and sight-seeing already. Where's Angel?"

Sue struggled into her one-piece seersucker fatigue dress and followed Jo out of the barracks, putting the finishing touches to her dressing as she went.

30

"She drew KP—which meant getting up at five o'clock, in case you've forgotten it during our recent soft existence."

"The poor kid—on our first day too."

"Don't feel too sorry for her. There's a flock of fellows over at the mess hall this morning, practically falling over each other to help us out. They wouldn't believe our cooks and bakers last night when they said they could manage all right without them."

That first day spent getting acquainted with their new station was one to be long remembered by all the members of the unit. They were delighted with their own quarters and touched by the efforts the men of the field had made for their pleasure as well as convenience. Everything was shiny, spanking new, from the collapsible tables of smooth pine finished in natural color and the red-topped stools of the mess hall to the many-windowed dayroom furnished with comfortable lounging chairs and divans, reading lamps, game tables, and writing desks. Sprays of flowering shrubs brought spring into the dayroom and spoke of welcome more intimately than any of the many other thoughtful touches the men had prepared.

What had been for so long a blank, waiting area became the scene of the kind of homemaking, settling-in activity that only women can set in motion. A fever of hair washing ran through the company; the laundry tubs were never empty and the electric irons were smoothed over miles of khaki shirts and skirts.

It was a wonderful feeling to sit in the sun and let the soft air of late April blow through freshly washed hair instead of sitting under a dryer within doors.

"Make the most of it, you lucky bums," said Sergeant O'Connell, stopping to chat for a moment with them as they drowsed together on the grass near their barracks.

"Meaning tomorrow we carry on as usual, heh?"

Sue peeked through her blond curls at the first sergeant and grinned at the open look of envy on her face.

"You'll know all in company meeting tonight," promised the sergeant. "Meanwhile the AWVS women will be here to show the noncoms around the field and you can do the errands at the PX for the rest of the gang."

"You mean Angel can't go sight-seeing with us?"

"Sorry. Working quarantine for two weeks, remember. No dates, no passes, until we're proven to be germfree. I was down at base headquarters this morning and I bet the fellows asked me a dozen times when the girls were coming over to work with them. They seem to like us around here and have a wonderful feeling about us. And, by the gods, we've got to keep that respect."

With a parting grimace of envy for their leisure, the sergeant moved briskly away. No sitting in the sun for her or the other noncoms and officers on duty.

"Boy! I wouldn't have her job for anything," Sue mumbled, rubbing her hair more briskly to hurry the drying process.

"No wonder the CO calls her her Rock of Gibraltar. She's a good gal. I hope we hear about our assignments tonight at company meeting. This house-cleaning stuff is all to the good, but I'm itching to get to work. You and I will get radio of some kind surely, but I'm dying to know what assignment Angel draws."

"So am I. We're pretty lucky at that, Josie, having a couple of stripes apiece to start with. Angel has to start right at the bottom. It's a pipe for us—about a job, I mean —having had special training."

"I wouldn't be too sure about that." Jo sounded thoughtful as she gathered up her towel and comb and rose to her feet. "We'd better get going if our tour of the field has to

32

This busy corner speaks for itself, for the WAC's behind desks and type-writers perform one of the most indispensable jobs in the armed services.

include PX purchases for our barracks. They'll be wanting everything from nail polish to candy bars. And I'm not worrying about our little Angela either. She'll probably have three stripes before we do."

Hours later Sue and Jo returned with other noncoms to the WAAC area laden down with purchases from the Post Exchange for other members of the company. They were filled with enthusiasm for what they had seen in their hasty tour of the post under the guidance of women from the AWVS, and thrilled with their reception at the PX.

"It's beautiful," Sue exulted, handing out items left and right to the girls who crowded around the returned shoppers.

"What's beautiful—the post or the PX?"

"Both, but we didn't get to see much of the post. We were too darn busy filling your orders. My gosh, we've practically spent the whole afternoon taking orders and getting them filled. The men at the PX were swell—said they'd sure be better prepared for us in a day or so when they've had a chance to stock up on nail polish and such. The officer in charge was a real duck, wasn't he, Jo?"

"I didn't notice you paying much attention to him. There I was, giving my all to wooden hangers, hand lotion, Kleenex, and soap flakes, while Sue here was off in the soda bar with a couple of GI Joe's named Johnny and Sam. All I got out of it was a sample from the coke machine bought with my own nickel."

"Soda bar!"

An envious sigh went up from the group gathered about the emissaries.

"I had to be polite, didn't I?" Sue laughed off her friend's teasing and pretended to go dreamy-eyed at the memory of her encounter. "Yup. Inlaid linoleum on the floors and a wonderfully decorated colorful archway separat-

34

Official U. S. AAF photo

A good switchboard operator is worth her weight in gold at any time or place; in the Air Forces she has to be super-excellent and she will be, if she is a WAC.

ing the store part of the PX from the soda bar and cafeteria. And a bomber crew still in flying togs sitting around a table in the cafeteria making plane flights with their hands. They didn't even buzz us."

Sue's voice was comically regretful as she made a ship with her hands, thumb against thumb, the fingers spread like wings, and sent it in a swooping dive over Angela's head.

"Did you see anything of the hangars or the runways or the ships?"

Angela's eyes were eager as she ducked to avoid the simulated flight of Sue's hands.

"Just a glimpse from the distance," Jo replied. The hangars are restricted territory, you know, and we can't go there unless we're sent on assignment. WAACs are strictly ground forces, unfortunately. Our flights will be flights of imagination. Period."

"Maybe so," said Sue, and Jo, noticing the glint in her eye, made a mental note not to let her get ahead of her if an opportunity should come to go aloft in one of the big ships that were constantly in the air over the field.

In answer to more eager questions the returned shoppers gave an animated account of their hurried sight-seeing trip with members of the AWVS who were assigned to the post as guides.

"There are two movies, and a huge gym where we can go to dance and swim, and a perfectly super Enlisted Men's Club, which we're invited to use, with its own snack bar and dance floor," said Sue, mentioning first the opportunities for off-duty recreation that had especially appealed to her.

"Don't forget the library," added Jo, smiling at Sue's light-footed gyrations to imaginary dance music. "It has lots of comfortable chairs, writing desks,. flowers, and reading lamps, to say nothing of what looked like a wonderful selection of books and magazines. Upstairs there is a special listening room for good records, and a technical library that I can't wait to dive into."

"As if we won't have enough of books by the time we plow through all the special-training sessions I hear we're going to have! It sure is attractive, though—I'll say that much. Nothing dry or dusty-looking about it. It has a couple of civilian librarians now, but I heard that some of us are going to be assigned to the job. I hope I'm not one of them, as attractive as the place is."

"No fear of that—you'd be about as appropriate in a library as a cricket. They ought to send you over to the EMC as recreation assistant. Except that that wouldn't be work for you, Susie."

Jo grinned at the look of scorn with which Sue received this suggestion.

"Not much. I want to be in the thick of things, even if I'm just a little cogwheel turning around among the great big wheels. Gosh, you should see the dispatcher's office, for instance, where all the pilots check in before and after flights. It was sure jammed today, being good flying weather. That's where I'd like to be—either there or up in the control tower."

"Did you go up into the tower?" asked Angela.

It was time for her to return to KP duties in the mess hall, but she was too generous to envy her two friends for their greater freedom because of the rating they had already achieved.

"No, we didn't. But that was about the only place we didn't at least stick our noses into—that and the photo lab. Come on, Jo. Don't tell 'em any more or there won't be any surprises left for them to discover tomorrow. Gosh, I haven't walked so much since I was a rookie."

As she and Jo went off to their own rooms Sue crossed

her fingers mentally—hoping that none of the Three B's would be assigned to the photo lab, which Johnny Samson had jeeringly called the "salt mines."

Jo felt a little bewildered by the bigness of the post and the variety of activities of which they had had a glimpse. In spite of Sue's airy recital about the warmth of the welcome they had received during their trip around the airfield, she had been conscious at times of a look of unease in the eyes of some of the soldeirs at work. Many of them had seemed in doubt as to whether to call them "ma'am" or by their rank. The majority had avoided conversation entirely except to answer an occasional question. She found herself wondering now how these men, who seemed so engrossed in their jobs, would adjust themselves to working shoulder to shoulder with the women whom they had to train to replace them.

Shortly before bed check that night Sue and Angela lingered in the dayroom—where the first company meeting had been held—to help Jo, who had been assigned as hostess in charge for a week, put things to rights before locking up and turning in the key to the orderly room. Many of the girls had stayed on after the meeting to discuss the assignments that had been read out to the assembled company, to sing around the piano, or to have a game of ping-pong or write letters.

On the whole, everyone had seemed satisfied with the job she had drawn and was eager to prove her mettle. The Three B's, however, were feeling somewhat subdued as they silently pushed furniture back into place, emptied ash trays, returned books and magazines to their shelves, and disposed of sprays of flowering shrubs that had begun to drop their blossoms on the polished floors.

Sue heard Angela humming softly to herself as she

A WAC mess sergeant in the kitchen of the consolidated mess at Stewart Field, New York.

worked, and wondered grumpily why she was feeling so cheerful.

At last the room was tidy and shining again and the three girls sank into one of the deep divans for a few moments before going back to barracks.

"My gosh, Angel, it burns me up to think of your having to spend your days like a mole underground in that smelly old photo lab."

At a look from Jo, Sue stopped herself from adding the term that Johnny had given the darkened rooms in which those who worked with photography had to spend a good share of their time. She looked searchingly at Angela, trying to make up her mind if her roommate was forcing herself to be cheerful or if she really was as satisfied over her assignment as she appeared outwardly to be.

"I only hope you are as tickled about your job as I am about mine," Angela assured her. "I had a little talk with Lieutenant Nolan tonight and she said she wouldn't be at all surprised if the training I get there makes it possible for me to get an overseas assignment—not as a photographer, of course, but as a laboratory technician back of the lines. She seems to know Lieutenant Cooper, the head of the department, quite well and she says he's really wonderful at his job. Oh, I know what they call the lab, all right, but I don't mind being sent to the 'salt mines' if I eventually get overseas."

"Well, I'll be darned!" Sue's eyes were round as she looked at Angela's dancing eyes. "Here I've been feeling sorry for you all evening and maybe I'm the one I should be grumbling about. I must say it doesn't sound very exciting for Jo and me to be going to work in the signal office. What good is our radio training going to do us in a spot like that? I wish Lieutenant Nolan was the commander of this company. She's swell."

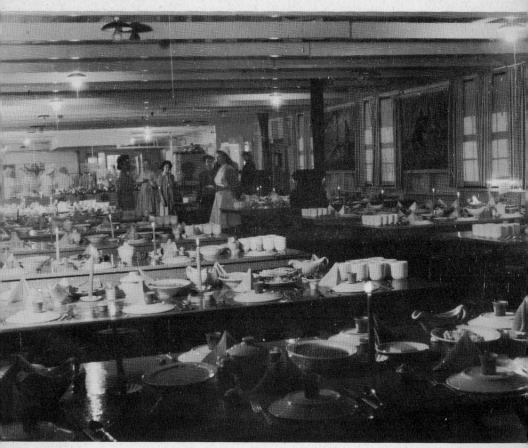

The WAC mess hall at Mitchel Field, New York, is an unusually attractive one with its paintings of WAC activities on its walls. Here it is shown with special fixings for Thanksgiving.

Sue yawned as she heaved herself up from the comfortable divan and, though she didn't say it aloud, her manner and emphasis made it plain that she wasn't a fervent admirer of Captain Cramer.

The barracks were abuzz that night until bed check with similar discussions about assignments, and the barracks police had their hands full before their final report was telephoned to the noncom in charge of quarters. By the time the CQ had finished her work and was able to stretch out on the cot set up in an office adjoining the orderly room, she was thankful that a regular working schedule would go into effect the next day.

On duty again at the entrance to the great airfield, Private First Class Johnny Samson ran his finger over the calendar tacked to the wall of the sentry room and stopped it at a date two weeks ahead.

"If everything goes per schedule, Johnny me boy, the end of that working quarantine will be the beginning of a wonderful friendship, I hope, I hope."

Remembering that Sue had two stripes on her sleeve to his one, he rubbed his chin reflectively. Here was a problem he hadn't run up against before.

"Gosh, I can't let my girl rate me," he thought uneasily.

But there was no resentment in his realization that such a thing could easily happen in this strange new Army where women for the first time worked with men on an equal basis. Nor, to tell the truth, did it occur to Johnny that the smiles Corporal Bates had bestowed on him that afternoon had been given with equal impartiality to Sam, to the bomber crew engrossed in their own business, to the attendants of the PX, and to the large chocolate soda to which he had treated her. That she had smiled, even for the moment, directly into his eyes was enough to straighten Johnny's shoulders and determine him to stop being sorry for himself because he had been assigned to the guard squad instead of radiowork, in which he had been interested since childhood. He thought of girls like his younger sister in the WAVEs and of Sue Bates doing the kind of work that a short time ago he would have thought girls were incapable of doing.

"It's a darn funny world," he mused, remembering the expression on Sam's face as he eyed on Sue's arm the rating that outranked Johnny's.

He turnoed to his fellow guard with a chuckle as a new thought struck him.

"At least we don't have to compete with the ladies on this job," he said, continuing his train of thought aloud.

The burly corporal of the guard looked at him in silence a moment and then a slow grin broke over his homely weather-beaten face.

"More's the pity," was his unexpected comment.

CHAPTER IV

Officers Are Also People

Captain Elizabeth Cramer walked briskly to her own snug quarters after the first company meeting held on the new post. Once her door had been closed behind her, her shoulders sagged wearily and a small wrinkle between her dark even eyebrows deepened to a furrow. It had been a strain giving out new assignments, knowing that a few members of her company were bound to be disappointed with the type of work in which they had been placed and that others were overly optimistic about what they hoped to accomplish immediately.

After all, only a few weeks separated them from a civilian existence in which discipline on the job and in personal life was vastly different from that of the Army. There were times, like this one, when the CO herself remembered with longing the wonderful Friday-night feeling that she had known as an instructor in a small woman's college. There was no week-end release in this job, she thought wearily; for, theoretically at least, an officer was on duty twenty-four hours a day.

Mechanically she removed her uniform, methodically putting each article in its proper place—a habit strongly formed long before she had undergone training in doing things, however small, the Army way. Not until her comfortable quarters were again in perfect order did she allow herself the luxury of stretching out on her bed to seek relaxation for her physical weariness. But her mind was unable to let go of the many details involved with the welfare of the hundred and more women under her care. The furrow between her eyes grew even deeper when a knock sounded at her door. She had hoped that she would be left in peace for a little while after this first day with its multitude of trying problems.

In response to her rather sharply spoken acknowledgment, the door was gently opened and the round smiling face of the company's mess and supply officer, Lieutenant Ruth Nolan, beamed at her.

Elizabeth sank back on her pillow with relief and, though her smile was not exactly cordial, she waved her visitor to a seat.

"Anything wrong?" she inquired.

She tried to sound lighthearted, but the worry line became almost a frown.

"Mind if I smoke?"

Unbuttoning her close-fitting blouse and pulling impatiently at her tie to loosen her shirt collar, Ruth sank back into a comfortable lounging chair with an air of such complete relaxation that Elizabeth envied her.

"I wish I could throw away care as easily as you do, Ruth. Anyone would think to look at you that you hadn't done a lick of work for a week, and yet the hardest part—physically at least—of all this settling in process has been on your shoulders. It's the strain of wondering whether these women, most of them mere kids and green as grass, will measure up to what is expected of us that gets me down."

Ruth lounged forward and held out the pack of cigarettes to Elizabeth, who shook her head reluctantly.

"You know I've given up smoking, for the duration," she said almost primly.

"Nuts."

Ruth leaned back in her chair and blew a few lazy rings at the ceiling before she continued.

"You did a swell job in company meeting tonight," she said at last. "I stayed and gossiped with a gang in the day-room for a while and they're raring to go—all of them. It's a swell bunch, if you ask me—which you haven't. They won't let you down, if that's what is worrying you."

"I'm not worrying. But, since this is the first group of WAACs to be assigned to this post, I do feel responsible for seeing that we give no one the slightest excuse for criticism. You must admit that that is a man-sized order."

"O.K., Sarah Maude. Wonder if kids still read *The Birds' Christmas Carol.* If I remember correctly, however, the little Ruggleses got along pretty well when put to the test at the Birds' fine big house, in spite of, and not because of, big sister's worrying."

Elizabeth raised herself on one elbow and looked at Ruth as if she were seeing her for the first time.

"Give me a cigarette," she said suddenly.

She caught the pack and the matches that Ruth tossed to her without changing her position and, plumping the pillows behind her head, achieved a position of comfort that almost matched that of her friend.

Ruth blew another perfect ring and stuck her finger through it before it widened and disappeared. Perhaps if she could help Elizabeth unbend a little, in private at least, she would realize that her schoolroom methods of handling the company just wouldn't work. The cigarette she was smoking, somewhat self-consciously after refusing one so curtly, was a good sign, Ruth thought, suppressing a smile. Bad habit, probably, but at least it made her seem more human.

"Did you notice the buzz of approval tonight when

Sergeant O'Connell announced it was O.K. to smoke in mess hall? Little things like that make a big difference, I think, in their feeling that the good old days of basic are behind them now."

"That's just what I'm afraid of—that they will forget too easily. The Air Force is pretty informal, it seems to me, in comparison to some Army posts."

"And I, for one, thank God for it," said Ruth fervently. "Maybe I'm prejudiced, with two brothers in the Air Forces and my own Ricky a bomber pilot with the Eighth Air Force; but the whole Corps is a team and it takes the finest human material and the best training we can give every member, as well as the finest ships we can build, to make the team work successfully. The type of discipline it demands may appear different from that in the other branches of the service, but it certainly isn't lax. I'm proud to think we're now a part of that team, even if we never step inside of a ship or even know the men who actually fly them."

A smile broke up Ruth's serious expression when she saw her superior officer suppress a yawn.

"I didn't mean to recite a creed or bore you at the end of a hard day," she apologized. "I was quoting Ricky, I guess, unconsciously."

"You're not boring me. You've made me unlax. I feel comfortably sleepy for the first time since I was handed this job, that's all. You're so capable and efficient and good-natured about everything that I never suspected you had a thought in the world about anything beyond mess and supply."

"With accent on the mess."

Ruth laughed as she leaned forward to pull a book from the small shelf of volumes on Elizabeth's desk.

"I wonder where that name came from anyhow. I ought to know, but for the first day or so before the rest of you got here the good old common definition, meaning 'state of disorder' or 'condition of unclean confusion,' pretty well described the situation."

"I used to teach Latin, you know, way back when; so I ought to be able to figure that one out, though I must say I've never wondered about it. I'm dead sure nobody ever saw your mess in a mess! It probably comes from the Latin *missum,* past participle of *mittere* to send—in other words, a 'dish sent to table.' There's an old French word *mes,* meaning dish. I know the term is still used in the Inns of Court, London, where four law students, or benchers, eat together."

Elizabeth's explanation was so unconsciously precise that Ruth would have been sorry she had mentioned the subject if she hadn't noticed the animation that lighted the dark eyes, which a moment before had been dull and disinterested. The sparkle was real enough, Ruth speculated. But why waste it on participles when people were so much more interesting? It would be real fun to open her eyes to that fact, if she could.

"Thanks, teacher. Participles sort of passed me by in my Latin days and I must say I don't 'missum' ordinarily. Excuse it please."

Ruth chuckled at the look of scorn with which Elizabeth received her play on words. She opened the book she had taken from the desk, and turned the pages until she found the passage she was looking for.

"I told you I was probably quoting Ricky or Tom or somebody when I was sounding off about the Air Forces being a team and so on. John Steinbeck said it in *Bombs Away,* and the thought stuck even if the words didn't—I remember this: '. . . in the Air Forces discipline is defined as that conduct of the individual which in a group best carries out the missions. And blind, unreasoning, unintelligent obedience does not accomplish this definition.' "

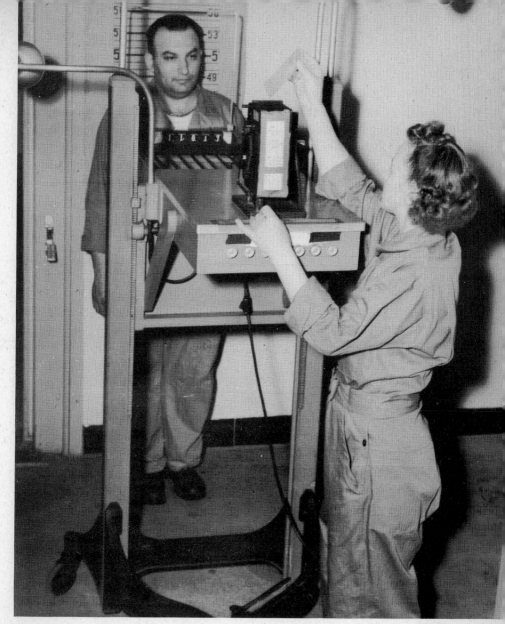

One of the many jobs of the WAC photo lab technician is the operation of this identification camera. Identification photographs are used for various types of passes.

As she returned the book to its place on the shelf, Elizabeth noted with satisfaction the care with which she handled it. Strange how little things in informal unguarded moments told you more about a person than any amount of purely businesslike contact with them did. She was beginning to think that Ruth wasn't as lazy mentally as she had thought she was. Moreover, she resented being dubbed "Sarah Maude" and "teacher" within the space of five minutes but wondered honestly if Ruth hadn't had cause on both counts. She didn't altogether approve of Ruth's informal manner with the enlisted personnel of the company. In fact, she had been meaning to speak to her about it—tactfully, of course.

. On the other hand, she had observed that she had not only the enthusiastic cooperation of every member of the staff under her but apparently their affection and respect as well. She remembered, with a pang of envy that hadn't been easy to acknowledge, the girls crowding around Ruth at the end of the company meeting, eager to discuss with her their expectations and hopes for the "training on the job" that would begin tomorrow. She had felt very lonely as she received their respectful good nights and went off alone to her own quarters.

There was something of this envy in her heart now as she broke the silence that followed Ruth's reading, but a sincere desire to be worthy of something more than respect gave a tinge of wistfulness to her voice.

"Did you gather, on the whole, that the girls were pleased with their assignments?"

"Sure thing. Some of them are a little scared about how the boys will treat them tomorrow—the timid ones, you know. And a few of them put up a big moan about being members of the Army Chair Corps—"

"The what?"

50

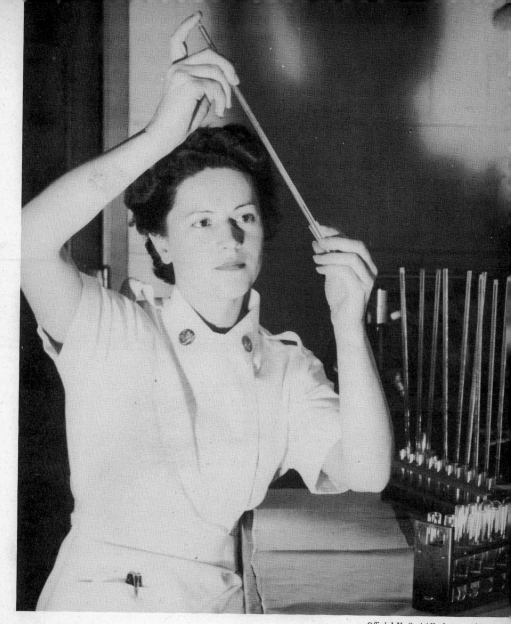

Accuracy is imperative in all work connected with hospital or laboratory work. A great variety of such work is ably done by WAC's. They assist in preparing antitoxins and vaccines, make up reports of hospital departments, supervise care of equipment.

Elizabeth sat up and clasped her arms around her knees, looking so much like an interested schoolgirl at that moment that Ruth chuckled aloud.

"Haven't you heard the famous Kelly Field Song? I copied down some of the words while the girls were singing them around the piano tonight. Don't be shocked now."

Ruth grinned as she pulled a scrap of paper from a pocket of her blouse and half read, half sang, the words that those assigned to officework had rendered so lustily a little earlier in the evening.

"Here we go, into the file case yonder,
Driving deep into the drawer.
Here it is, buried away down under
That stuff we've been searching for.
Off we go into the CO's office,
Where we get one helluva roar.
We live by miles of paper files,
But nothing can stop the Army Chair Corps.

And more of the same, such as

"With dictionary we're stationary,
Nothing can move the Army Chair Corps."

As she tucked the paper away in her pocket, Ruth saw with relief that Elizabeth was regarding her with amusement.

"Takes me back to some of the crazy songs we sang during OCS. Remember the one about

"The biscuits that they serve us
They say are mighty fine,
But one fell off the table
And killed a pal o' mine.

And several others even less refined."

52

"Well, they all helped to blow off steam, didn't they? When I left, the same bunch was singing Brahms' 'Cradle Song' led by that cute little piece Angela Borelli. She'll soon have them licked into shape as a company chorus or I miss my guess."

"Is she the slender fair-haired corporal assigned to the signal office?"

"No, that's Sue Bates. Angela is a pal of hers and with Corporal Josephine Barrows makes up a trio known as the Three B's."

"Oh, yes, I know her now. I wish I had your memory for faces. I know their names and records, but I haven't had time to put all the faces and names together yet."

"It's hard to miss those three—they went through basic together and haven't gotten over their glee at being reunited here, for Sue and Jo were sent to radio school while Angel sort of marked time on temporary assignments."

"How does she like the idea of working in the base photo lab? I know she hasn't had any special training in photography, but then none of our girls have had and Lieutenant Cooper is frantic for help. He's just lost eight of his best men and is fit to be tied. I'm afraid the girls who work with him are in for a bad time of it, until they get used to the work."

"Don't worry; they'll make the grade all right, once they learn his bark is worse than his bite. The girls are a little bewildered at the moment, being as green as they are; but I think you and the personnel officer made canny choices for that particular job. Angela, especially. She has her heart set on going overseas and I wouldn't be surprised if she gets to go, eventually. She's deceptively modest and mild, but a real leader in a very quiet, unobtrusive fashion."

"I'm glad to hear you say that, Ruth. I'll confess Lieutenant Cooper bothered me a little. He was pretty outspoken over having to replace his personally trained men with four dumb women who haven't even been bad amateur photographers and whose conception of film is something the tooth-paste commercials talk about. I'm quoting him, you understand."

"He ought to be grateful. He won't have so many bad habits to get rid of. I'm betting on Angela, just the same, to change his tune. You can't blame the man for being sore. His work requires a lot more than mechanical skill and it takes a long time even to acquire that. These first few weeks are going to be tough going—tough on all of us until we learn the ropes; and tough on the men who are responsible to turn out the work, regardless. It's our job to bolster up the girls' confidence when they need it and to let them know we believe in them and trust them, in a big way. That's more important than fussing at them for little things, such as chewing gum and talking too loud or making eyes at a good-looking soldier."

"But little things, as you call them, can create a wrong impression of the Corps too," said Elizabeth stubbornly.

An impatient retort was on the tip of auburn-haired Ruth's tongue; but she swallowed it quickly, deciding that she had said enough for one evening.

"O.K., boss. But don't forget the enlisted gals *are* the Corps, and that they are just as jealous of its reputation as its officers—maybe more so. Golly Moses! It's late, and I've got umpteen reports to make out before I can hit the hay. I swear there are times when I envy these kids. I bet they have more fun by a darn sight than we do. As much as I hate to admit it, some Army men look on us WAAC officers as glorified housekeepers.

"And how some of those boys down at headquarters love to kid us! Just this afternoon I answered the telephone and a crisp voice said 'Major Brownell speaking.' (He's Supply

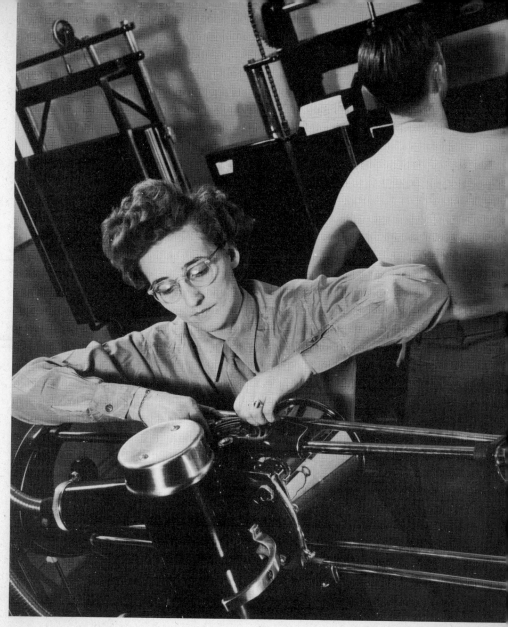

WAC gives chest X-Ray. The X-Ray department of a base hospital offers interesting and exciting possibilities to a WAC who appreciates the importance of this vital aid to modern medicine. WAC's assist in taking X-Rays and develop X-Ray films.

Officer, you know.) 'I just wanted to check up on your supply of WAAC girdles and bras, Lieutenant.' I stuttered a few 'sirs' into the phone until I realized it was Captain Randall of Public Relations trying to pull another fast one on me. I bet he lies awake nights trying to think up new gags.

"So far I've caught on before he's hung up; but one of these days some major or colonel will really call up about something that sounds like one of Randall's jokes and I'll probably be court-martialed for what I'm thinking, even if I manage not to say it! I'm glad I was brought up with brothers. Otherwise I might not understand the male sense of humor."

"You'll have to help me, then; for I haven't any brothers, worse luck. On the whole I have found the men very considerate and cooperative. In fact, a few of them seem almost too concerned about the girls' being overworked."

"I know that kind, too, and don't be taken in by them. Mark my words, Elizabeth, it won't be long before they become one of your big problems. Captain So'n'so will call up and inquire benevolently if you haven't been giving his precious WAAC Whosis more than her share of KP lately, or Major Big will inform you that he has decided to let Auxiliary Whatsis start her furlough a couple of days earlier than you said she could."

"But surely they understand that our regulations apply to every member of the detachment, without favoritism, Ruth. I think you're just thinking up problems."

"Want to put a bet on it? I wasn't in the business world ten years for nothing, my love. Not that I'm blaming the men, for the most part."

"You surely don't mean that any of our WAACs would try to get around an officer in an underhanded manner like that?"

Elizabeth sounded so indignant that Ruth chortled over such innocence.

"My lands, child—even WAACs are women, God bless 'em. If you don't mind, I'll just pretend you didn't ask that question."

Ruth rose reluctantly and peered at herself in the mirror while she yanked her tie into place with a groan.

"I have to laugh when some of my friends moan about the dangers of all the Army regimentation we are exposing ourselves to. If regimentation was all it is cracked up to be, there wouldn't be any practical jokers or overprotective Big-Hearts to get in our hair! Personally I'd rather have the smart guys and the softhearted regulation busters, even if they are a headache.

"Wonder what it will feel like to have an untrammeled neckline again? I didn't mean to talk your ear off, when you're so dog-tired," she added apologetically as she opened the door. "I guess I needed to blow off a little steam, so thanks again."

Elizabeth rubbed her ears and smiled at her departing guest with mingled shyness and gratitude.

"My ears needed to be talked off. And maybe they took in more than you really intended they should."

"But I didn't mean—" began Ruth, looking so dismayed that Elizabeth's smile turned into quiet laughter.

"Come again—and often. I don't always think in terms of Latin past participles; honestly I don't."

The company commander's face was serious but her eyes were not, and for once Ruth was at a loss for words.

"Good night, boss," she said briefly, and closed the door softly behind her.

"My gosh, she's human. And, what's more, I like her," she thought gleefully as she hurried off to tackle the stack of reports and requisitions waiting for her.

"Trouble with you is you talk too much," she scolded herself silently. "Hereafter you stick to potatoes and canned goods and GI blankets, my lass, and let the CO handle the intangibles. . . . Whatever got into me anyhow, sending up a spout like Moby Dick about discipline et cetera?"

Irritated with herself as the echo of her words came back to her, Lieutenant Nolan glared at the ruled forms on her desk. This was the part of her work that she intensely disliked—forms, forms, forms, millions of them.

"Every job has a few flies in the amber," she reminded herself as her pen began its laborious journey over the stack of papers under her hands.

While Lieutenant Nolan worked under a well-shaded light in her own quarters, Captain Cramer's windows were dark; but her mind was even busier than that of her junior officer as she reviewed her brief career as commander of a WAAC company. She knew that Ruth was too guileless to have spoken of nagging about personal details as implied criticism of her, but in all fairness she had to admit that some of her random remarks might well suit her. With characteristic honesty she determined to try to place responsibility for individual conduct and progress where it belonged —on the shoulders of the noncoms.

"Channels work both ways," she thought as her eyes grew heavier and heavier. "Here I've been worrying about the girls forgetting all the things they learned in basic training, while I've been turning by back on the primary lessons dinged into us at OCS."

For the first time since she had been put in command of her company, a practical realization of her job began to take form in her mind.

"It's like working on a jigsaw puzzle," she thought sleepily. "I know what the picture ought to be when it's finished, but it takes quite a while to fit all the pieces to-

gether. Anyhow, we've all got one big thing in common—
for it's 'training on the job' for officers too. . . . And don't
think your little darlings don't know it."

A final relaxing yawn ended in a smile as this strangely
comforting thought brought the first immediate and dream-
less slumber that the weary young company commander had
known for several nights.

CHAPTER V

Off to the "Salt Mines"

Lieutenant Cooper swept a pile of papers to one side of his desk with an impatient gesture, picked up a pencil and began to run it through his fingers as he faced the four girls seated before him. He looked at them, one at a time, so appraisingly that each girl in turn began to feel as if she were an insect being examined under a microscope. His polished spectacles reflected the light from the window at his back, making his keen gray eyes seem sharper than he meant them to be.

"Tap. Plop. Tap. Plop."

The rhythmic sound of the pencil striking the bare patch on the cluttered desktop, first the sharp tap of the point and then the softer accent of the erasered end, began to get on the nerves of the four silent figures seated in front of the head of the base photo laboratory. With an effort Angela kept her eyes fixed on the lieutenant's face instead of following the course of the yellow pencil as the long slender fingers reversed it expertly and brought it down, head and point, to the same exact spot on the scarred wood.

The three other girls, who with Angela had been assigned to Lieutenant Cooper, seemed mesmerized by the flash of yellow as it rose and fell between the nervous fingers of the department head.

Involuntarily Angela smiled as the lieutenant's eyes began their scrutiny of her, and to her surprise a twinkle appeared in the steady eyes regarding her. To everyone's relief the monotonous tapping of the pencil ceased as Lieutenant Cooper leveled it in Angela's direction and broke the silence that had seemed longer than it really was.

"What's your name, again?"

"Angela Borelli, sir."

"Italian?"

"I am an American, sir."

"Oh, sure, sure, I know that. Your folks Italian?"

"My father and mother came from northern Italy, sir. From Milan."

"Mm. Do you speak Italian?"

"A little, sir."

"Have you ever been in Italy?"

"No, sir," said Angela, beginning to wonder why the lieutenant had singled her out for this kind of questioning. "But I would like to be sent there on overseas duty, if possible, sir," she added impulsively.

"You might as well get that idea out of your head right now, young lady. We've lost four batches of expert men to date, and most of them I trained from the ground up. If I can lick you women into any kind of shape you're going to stay put. So if you aren't willing to proceed on that basis we might as well know it now. After going over your records and from talking to you this morning, I gather you are all green as grass as far as knowing anything about this work is concerned."

Lieutenant Cooper leaned back in his chair and tapped his chin with the end of the pencil.

His air of gloom, strangely enough, appealed to the girls' sense of humor and brought back some of their self-confidence that had been slowly oozing away in the last hour. In spite of his blunt words they began to take more interest

61

in being trained for the job to which they had been assigned. None of them, except Angela, had been very enthusiastic about it up until this point.

The lieutenant's detailed explanation during a cursory tour of the photo lab had left them bewildered and doubtful about ever being able to satisfy his exacting standards. No one ventured a reply to his last remark, but their aroused pride was apparent in the four pairs of eyes that regarded their new department head. Four young backs stiffened ever so slightly as Lieutenant Cooper sat forward in his chair and pushed the pencil so impatiently to one side that it flew off the edge of the desk and landed at Angela's feet. Stooping swiftly, she picked it up and laid it quietly on the desk.

"Thank you. And don't wait on me," he grumbled, rumpling his brown hair with an almost embarrassed gesture. "We've got too much to do around here to waste time on a lot of fiddle-faddle. On the job we work like beavers and to hell with everything but turning out the best damn job we're capable of. From now on you aren't even women to me—you're four pairs of hands and legs. And before you get through you'll wish, as I do, that you each had a pair of heads too.

"I guess that's all for now. I can't start you in today— you might get those pretty uniforms all splashed up. Be here tomorrow prepared to plunge in. If you haven't got your zoot suits yet, I guess I can find some coveralls around here for you. You'll get dishpan hands from dabbling in the developing and fixing tanks, and eyestrain from peering at negatives, and aching backs from standing around on your feet all day. On the other hand, you'll have the satisfaction of knowing that the guys you're replacing are going to do one of the most important jobs there is on actual battle fronts.

"I suppose you haven't any idea about the important role photography plays in war, have you?"

"My youngest brother is a tail gunner in the South Pacific, sir, and acts as cameraman too. So I know a little, at least, about it. For a while he was a member of a reconnaissance unit. Sometimes they even developed their pictures while in motion and dropped them to land forces to give them up-to-the-minute information on enemy positions as our troops moved in."

Lieutenant Cooper looked at Angela intently as she spoke, noting the animation in her deeply blue eyes and her complete ease of manner.

"Yes, the camera is one of our most important factors in Intelligence operations—a real super Mata Hari. To make a bombing mission effective, photo reconnaissance and interpretation must come first. In addition, of course, the camera is indispensable in making maps, in recording battle actions, and in hundreds of other ways. I'll tell you more about our uses of photography—in peace as well as war—sometime, if you'd be interested."

"We'd also like to hear about your own experiences in North Africa, sir," said Jean eagerly. "Lieutenant Nolan told us you were there for several months."

"So I was, as a news cameraman. Then I joined the Army and have been stuck with this job ever since. I wish you could have seen some of the holes we often had to develop our stuff in behind the front. Once we dug our darkroom out of the side of a hill and every damn thing about it was homemade. Our safety lamp was rigged up from an electric torch and a tail-light salvaged from a bombed jeep, and we made our film-developing tank from bomb cases. We cut gasoline tins in half, the long way, to use for developing and fixing trays. Our running water flowed into our cave through some piping taken from the hydraulic system

63

of a dismantled B-17, and on the end of the pipe we fixed a wine-barrel spigot to shut the water off with. All our chemicals were kept in wine bottles, coke bottles—anything we could lay our hands on.

"Came hell or high water—and we had plenty of both—we turned out the work though, so we ought to be able to handle this job without any trouble."

"If it's all right with you, sir, we'd like to come back after chow and look around some more. We're very anxious to get started, and I'm sure we could keep from getting in the way of the men, sir."

Angela glanced confidently at her three companions, who indicated they were in agreement with her suggestion.

The lieutenant slapped the desktop with an open palm as he rose briskly to his feet and gave all four girls an expansive smile to show his appreciation of their good will.

"Fine, fine," he said, characteristically repeating the word for emphasis. "I won't be here this afternoon—have a little aerial job to do—but Sergeant Martin will take care of you. I'll speak to him. Make yourselves at home, but don't go busting into the lab without first looking through the mousehole in the wall outside. What is it, Corporal . . . The lieutenant hesitated over the name for a moment, snapping his fingers impatiently. "Don't tell me—I know it. . . . Johnson. I've got it—Corporal Johnson."

He shot a forefinger in the corporal's direction and looked pleased with himself.

"No, sir," said Corporal Hanson, suppressing a smile.

Lieutenant Cooper looked very boyish as he curved his long forefinger, then straightened it toward Angela.

"Borelli—I know that's right—Hanson, Johnson, and Matson. Sounds like a nursery rhyme. If you're not Johnson, you're either Hanson or Matson. You're Matson."

"No, sir."

Official U. S. AAF photo

WAC's who become base photo laboratory technicians must learn to use cameras of various kinds, and are often given interesting and important "shooting" assignments on the ground. They do not do aerial photography.

But Mary Hanson couldn't resist a giggle at the young officer's look of comical concentration.

"Ha! Then you've got to be Hanson."

He cocked his head slightly to one side as he surveyed the three "sons," trying to fix the right name for each in his mind. All three girls were of medium height; all were blonde, and a slow blush was beginning to creep into the cheeks of each fair-skinned face.

The lieutenant wagged his head from side to side and looked appealingly at Angela.

"As like as three peas in a pod," he said sadly. "Of course I can always tell Hanson by her stripes, but Johnson and Matson—"

"I'm Jean Matson, sir. And may I ask you a question, please, sir?"

"Yes, yes. But do you girls *have* to bring out quite so many sirs all in one sentence? What do you want to know?"

"Will we ever have a chance to do any aerial photography—I mean after we've had lots of training, of course, sir."

"Not a chance in this world."

After a keen glance at his questioner, as if to fix her name in his memory, Lieutenant Cooper beckoned the girls to follow him into the room adjoining his office.

He waved a hand toward the aerial cameras and photographic equipment in one corner of the room and looked down at his four apprentices benevolently. They were becoming used to his abruptness by this time and were fully enjoying their wholly informal induction.

"That's just part of the equipment an aerial man has to lug aboard a plane," he explained. "Believe me it would take a Powerful Katinka to move it, and a woman just isn't strong enough to do the job. That's one reason anyhow, and the other reasons haven't anything to do with brains or skill.

A photographer at the front is a soldier with a camera instead of a gun, or sometimes with both, whether he's in the air or on the ground.

"Believe me it's no job for a woman, no matter how good a photographer she might be. I'm not a woman hater, you know. Just realistic. And I expect you women to be realistic too. You'll have a chance to learn how to use cameras all right, both in the studio and on special assignments. There may even be times when you'll have to hop out on the double-quick to get shots of a crash landing or even a movie star."

The lieutenant grinned wickedly when he saw the girls' faces light up at the mention of activities other than those connected with the work in the laboratory.

"But meanwhile you've got a lot to learn—first principles first, is my motto. You'll even have a chance later on to show whether you have that sixth sense that a good technician needs to be an artist. That's something you're born with, I reckon. Plenty of training and practice can help to bring it out, but it can't put it in you if you don't have the flare—the instinct—the feeling."

Lieutenant Cooper smiled apologetically as he closed the door of the equipment room.

"Don't get me wrong, now. I'm not expecting any of you to be artists. God forbid."

He stood in the doorway of his office looking after the four trim figures until they had left the building, wondering if he had been too hard on them in the first interview. He wasn't too cheerful over the prospect of having to break in four new workers; still he could bank on not having them sent on overseas assignments as soon as he had them trained.

"And that, my friend, is some comfort, such as it is," he muttered as he went in search of Sergeant Martin to tell him to keep an eye on the girls that afternoon.

"Four dead ducks, Dan, and we're starting from scratch with them. There isn't even an amateur camera crank in the bunch."

"All the better, if you ask me. Leave it to me, boss— I'll give 'em the works, if they do turn up."

But Dan sounded so doubtful that Lieutenant Cooper looked at him derisively.

"Boy, they'll be here! They were ready to spit tacks at me when they left, which is just the way I wanted them to feel. You'd better get yourself a good lunch, Sarge. You're going to need it, if I know Hanson, Matson, Johnson, and Borelli."

"Thought you said they were a bunch of dead ducks," grumbled Dan, fidgeting over the prospect of dealing with four very determined young women in the lieutenant's absence.

It certainly wasn't the way he would have described the newcomers, not by a long shot, he thought gloomily.

"And so they are, technically speaking, Dannie me boy. From the photogenic point of view . . ."

"Hum," agreed Dan reluctantly, listening to the lieutenant's soft whistling as he packed up his gear for the afternoon's assignment.

The mild-mannered, hard-working sergeant aimed a savage kick at a cardboard carton that had been left in the middle of the drying-room floor and restrained an impulse to retrieve the box from under the table, where he had sent it flying. His sense of order was outraged by small evidences of disorder here and there throughout the rooms; but, short-handed as they were, it was impossible to turn out the work, let alone keep everything in the apple-pie order that meant efficiency as well as pleasure to the eye.

" 'Give 'em the works,' says the lieutenant, meaning 'Give 'em a complete course in how to run a photo lab,' I

Official U. S. AAF photo

WAC's who become base photo lab technicians learn to be expert in handling all modern equipment such as this self-adjusting enlarger.

suppose. Be jabbers, I'd like to give 'em each a broom and a scrubbing brush."

With a scowl at his wrist watch Sergeant Martin clumped off to chow, knowing that the interruption of his afternoon's plans would mean working until well past midnight to catch up with his schedule.

When he returned half an hour later he was surprised to find that the four girls were on hand and waiting for him. They had removed their hats, gloves, and shoulder bags and were looking at some of the excellent aerial photographs and maps that hung on the walls of the well-lighted order office that also served as workroom and lounge.

Dan noticed with embarrassment that the long tabletop was streaked with dust and littered with magazines and un-emptied ash trays, but the girls seemed oblivious to everything except the photographs they were studying.

"We're sort of proud of those photos of New York Harbor and the Battery," he admitted, pleased with their evident appreciation of them. "They were taken before the war of course. The chances of hitting the right atmospheric conditions for good shots of those towers and canyons are about one in a million.

"Sorry things are in such a mess around here. We've been so darned busy in this place and fellows have been shipped out so fast we can't even get the work turned out, let alone keep things in order. We lost eight good men last week—all in one fell swoop."

Dan sent a shy swift glance over the four figures in uniform as if to apologize for his blunt words.

"Better put us to work then, Sergeant—the quicker the better. The proportion is a little high of course—four WAACs to replace eight men—but maybe we'll surprise you."

Angela smiled at the sergeant so winningly that he

70

Official U. S. AAF photo

WAC photo lab technicians at work in the "dark room," as the photographic laboratory where negatives and prints are processed is called. The WAC in the foreground is operating a contact printer—making prints which are the same size as the negative. In the back another WAC is washing the prints after they have been developed and "fixed."

pinched his chin speculatively as he looked with new interest at the four friendly faces in front of him.

"Maybe you will at that. But Lieutenant Cooper said—"

"We have a pretty good idea what the lieutenant had to say," Mary Hanson broke in quickly. "He also told us there were some coveralls around somewhere that we could use until our issue comes through. You dig them up for us and we'll dig in for you. After all, why waste a whole afternoon?"

With a helpless gesture of defeat Dan ducked out of the room and soon returned with an armful of acid-stained but clean coveralls, which he dumped onto the table.

"Remember, you asked for it," he said as he backed out of the room, a broad grin on his face.

"Give us five minutes," Mary called after him, but Dan was already on his way to warn the men in the laboratory that the WAACs had taken things into their own hands.

They needed little direction for the job of cleaning up that they had taken on voluntarily, for they found plenty to do. Angela tackled the small closetlike workroom where developing and fixing formulas were made up. Though the odor of acids and chemicals bothered her at first, she gradually became accustomed to it as she put clean papers on the shelves, scrubbed sink and worktable until they shone, and rearranged the supplies and replaced labels under Dan's direction until his grin of approval was reward enough for her aching muscles and stained fingers. She liked the slow-spoken sergeant's ability to explain simply the formulas used in the work of the laboratory. By the time the chemical room had been restored to order she was surprised at how much she had learned in the process of house cleaning.

In the studio, where Jean and Mary scrubbed and dusted, Dan demonstrated the uses of the different cameras and the lighting systems. He showed them how to set up a crypto-

72

graph in a holder that was used for all identification cards and passes. From a partitioned tray filled with white letters he had Jean select those that spelled her own name, adding figures for her serial number. Holding the cryptograph in front of her chest, he posed her as subject while Mary focused the small camera used for this special purpose and pressed the bulb.

"You'll get plenty of practice with that little black box," promised Dan. "It records every face on the post, from every GI Joe—and Jill," he added slyly, "to top-ranking brass hats. This won't be a picture your best beau will wear next his heart, Jean; but, by golly, you'll carry it next to yours. Once it's fastened to your little blue identification card you'd better hang on to it—or else!

"Now we'll put it through the works—develop the negative, make a print of it in the contact room, and then enlarge it, just for fun, so you can see the self-focusing enlarger do its stuff."

By the time the afternoon was over, Dan seemed to feel as much satisfaction in what had been accomplished as did his four new helpers. He looked from one tired—dust-streaked girl to the other and a slow smile wrinkled the corners of his gray eyes.

"I hope we didn't work you too hard on your first day," he began apologetically. "I don't know what the boss will say when he hears I've had you scrubbing and scouring all afternoon."

"We asked for it, remember. Besides, we've learned a lot already," said Mary earnestly. "A picture of the work here has begun to emerge out of the fog we were in this morning. It was something like seeing Jean's face appearing from a plain piece of white paper when it was put into the developing solution."

Jean pulled her demonstration photograph from the

73

pocket of her coveralls and made a comical face as she looked at it.

"A mug if ever I saw one," she said, with a shudder. "Posterity is in for some good laughs if this is a fair sample of your studio art, Sergeant."

"I'll show you some real portraits tomorrow," Dan promised. "You'd be surprised how fussy some of our subjects are. But we try to please them, even if they expect the traditional birdie to sing like a Chinese nightingale."

"Well, I had fun too," said Margaret Johnson, "even if those fellows did mess up my nice clean room working on their old map mosaic. I wondered why you needed such a big table in here, but I know now. It's quite a job fitting all those sections together to make one big map. Those boys certainly are good at it. I even helped a little bit," she added proudly.

"Good for you."

Dan chuckled quietly, remembering the resentment that those same two map makers had shown when they heard that four women were to be added to the staff of the photo lab.

"I take it, then, you don't mind being condemned to the 'salt mines'?" he asked as he turned to leave.

"Not any more," Angela assured him. "And, from now on, anybody'd better smile when they say those words to us."

When Dan had gone and the girls were busy cleaning up for their long walk home, Margaret admitted that she didn't get the point about "salt mines."

"Out in Utah, where I come from, salt is taken right out of Great Salt Lake—acres and acres of it scooped up like snow when the water in the drying ponds has evaporated. What is a salt mine, really?"

Angela looked at Margaret in amazement before answering her question.

"Do you mean to say you've never heard of the great

74

"Dark room" work—developing film and making prints and enlargements of photographs taken in the air as well as on the ground—is an important phase of the work done at any Army Air Forces base. WAC's who do this kind of work are called photo lab technicians. In an army school for photo lab technicians they learn a myriad of things about photography —how to take pictures, mix chemicals, process negatives and prints, and how to make mosaics.

Siberian salt mines to which men were condemned as punishment? They worked underground like slaves and hardly ever saw the light of day again. I will admit this place depressed me this morning, with all the locked doors behind which developing was going on, the eerie yellow light of the printing room, and the pad of rubber-shod feet on floor boards and the almost constant sound of running water. But I didn't feel any of that this afternoon. I even rather like the sharp smell of the chemicals by this time, though it bothered me at first."

"It's a good thing you do, then, because I heard Dan tell one of the men in the developing room that he had a new assistant for mixing formulas."

"That would suit me just fine. Good practice for me when I find myself in one of those homemade laboratories behind the front lines that Lieutenant Cooper described to us."

"You have a one-track mind, haven't you? Lieutenant Cooper was almighty emphatic about our making up our minds to stay put, wasn't he?"

"Yes, he was," agreed Angela, with a smile. "But I have an idea he won't 'stay put' himself—at least not if he can help it. I can dream, can't I?"

Jean took one more look at her new GI photograph before she tucked it into her shoulder bag and followed the other girls out of the building.

"Yes, you can dream if you want to. Me, I'm going to bed tonight and treat myself to a nice little nightmare. And, if this is the way I really look, it ought to be a humdinger."

CHAPTER VI

Yonder, Unlimited

"Here we go, into the bright blue yonder," hummed Sue as she and Jo stepped out briskly on their long walk to the signal office, where they were to report for duty for the first time.

"Yonder is right," agreed Jo, pausing for a moment to take in the full beauty of the flowering shrubs that lined the winding drive leading from their own area to the main part of the post.

"No lingering or loitering en route, remember," said Sue in so exact an imitation of Captain Cramer's crisp tones that Jo chuckled.

"She's not so bad. I caught her passing a wink to Lieutenant Nolan this morning in the orderly room—so help me."

"I'd have to see it to believe it, and even then I'd think she was trying to bat out a cinder or something."

"Just the same, she has what it takes to make a good CO—if we give her a chance. She's a little shy, I think, and nervous about the impression we're going to make in these first weeks. But who isn't? We'll learn, in time, now that we're actually on the job—or soon will be. Where is this darn place anyhow? I'm all turned around."

"What do we do in the infantry? We march, we march, we march," sang Sue under her breath. "And that goes for the Air Forces, too, apparently. Let's see—fifteen minutes' walk four times a day adds up to just about four miles, doesn't it? Me, who used to think a five-minute walk from the subway to the office was cruelty to animals. Why, I thought feet were sort of in the same class as the human appendix—you had 'em, but what good were they?"

At the edge of a wide macadam road the two girls had to pause while a huge army truck thundered by, followed by a long line of identical vehicles rumbling along as evenly spaced as if they had been measured off with a ruler. Regulations forbade walking through a convoy, so they had to wait until the fifty trucks or more had passed before they continued on their way.

"Kind of hard on an old New York jay walker, isn't it?" said Jo when the road again was empty and they hurried toward a huge red brick building topped by a glass-enclosed control tower. "We'll have to remember to make allowances for convoys hereafter. Take a deep breath, Corporal. Here we are. I hope that nice fatherly major who welcomed us yesterday on our orientation tour remembers that we're supposed to work here. I'll be glad when our first few weeks are over. I hate not knowing just what I'm supposed to do."

Sue looked at her companion in amazement. Was it possible that Jo, the most poised and self-sufficient member of the whole company, was actually nervous at this point?

"You've never done a job before, have you?" she asked, pausing for a moment outside of the signal office.

"No. I finished at the university in the middle of the year and signed up immediately afterward. You go first." Jo grinned apologetically and gave Sue a slight push toward the door. "Go on, hard-boiled businesswoman. I'll be all right once the plunge is over."

"O.K., Josie. A job's just a job to me. They're all alike —business or Army—and you've got to make your own

Official U. S. AAF photo

These WAC photo lab technicians take time off from their duties of processing negatives and prints to mount a map. Sometimes they are called upon to make mosaics which show the topography of a given area.

place in 'em usually. First few days you feel like a fifth wheel, until people get used to having you around, and then before you know it you're in to your neck. Talk up to the major, now; you made a real impression on him yesterday, I noticed."

But the kindly major was nowhere to be seen and the sergeant in charge seemed to be completely surprised by the appearance of two new members in his department. In fact, his embarrassment was so acute that Jo forgot her own qualms and suggested that they spend the day in observation until specific responsibilities had been found for them.

"I'll have one of the boys show you around," offered the sergeant with such evident relief as he returned to his own work that Sue couldn't resist an "I-told-you-so" poke at Jo.

As the long hours without any specific responsibilities dragged on, gloom began to settle on the two girls who had started the day with such expectations.

"As far as I can discover they just don't need two gals with our kind of training, Josie," confessed Sue as they sorted a heap of teletype messages, trying to make the job last as long as possible.

"I'm afraid you're right. From Sergeant Langtree's description of the main radio station, miles from the base, I can't picture us being of the least possible use there. What do we know about dynamos bigger than this whole office? We'd better have a good talk with the CO, if things go on as they have today."

"You can't always tell about first days of course, but this one has been about the most frustrating one I've ever had— and I've known a few at that, back in good old civilian days."

Sue sounded so solemn that Josephine was sorry she had given voice to her own discouragement. It would have been a relief to have Sue go into one of her famous grumbling

With marked ease, this WAC wheels a high-powered tractor as it tows
a huge airplane into position for a flight. This is one of many tasks the
WAC's do quietly and effectively at busy airbases.

monologues, but Jo realized suddenly that Sue never grumbled about anything but trifles concerned with personal discomfort. She felt they had no right to regard their assignment with such pessimism after a few hours' trial, but she was unable to shake off the mood of futility that had seized them both.

When the long first day was over, the girls started off to their own area eager to exchange experiences with other members of the company.

"I wonder how Angel made out with the 'Prince of Darkness,'" said Sue. "That's what O'Connell called him. Remember? I'll bet he was on hand to put those photo-lab kids through a course of sprouts. If they were left cooling their heels, the way two expert radio mechanics I could mention were, I'll drink a pint of developing fluid. My face hurts from trying to look intelligent and interested every time Sergeant Lankylegs threw an agonized glance in my direction. Wonder what happened to our friend the major? The first chance I get I'm certainly going to tell him we didn't come here to sort teletype messages."

"Like fun you will. There's a little item called 'channeling' in the Army. Remember?"

"Yes, I remember—Corporal Bates to First Sergeant O'Connell—O'Connell to the CO—the CO to So'n'so— So'n'so to Whosis and Whatsis—and in six months maybe Bates can get her nice long tail back again."

"Oh, it's not as bad as all that," Jo protested. "Now that the first day is over, maybe it wasn't as bad as we thought it was. Even Sergeant Langtree thawed out when he said good night."

"Sheer relief, I betcha. But if he thinks he's been handed a couple of glorified Western Union messengers, he's got another think coming. That's the fifth time today we've saluted that roving-eyed second looey," Sue muttered when

82

First Sergeant

Official U. S. AAF photo

The scene is the busy orderly room of the WAC Detachment at Stewart Field, New York. Here all administrative matters pertaining to WAC's are handled. Shown, left to right are: (foreground) the company clerk; (background) the supply sergeant; one of the administrative lieutenants and the first sergeant of the detachment.

they were beyond earshot of an officer who returned their meticulous salutes with one equally snappy. "He's cute, but I'll bet Johnny Samson's more fun. And I don't mean sour grapes, either. What do you hear from Bill, by the way?"

"He's been made a first lieutenant and is somewhere in Africa. I had a letter at noon, but of course he can't say much about what he's doing."

"Remind me to look him up when I go overseas," said Sue airily. "Speaking of letters, wasn't it fun to hear from Ann Dudley? As soon as we're out of this blessed quarantine we'll take her up on that date, won't we? Why do you suppose it's called working quarantine, anyhow? Anything but, if you ask me, working elbow to elbow with the fellows all day."

"Did you say working?"

"Speaking for publication, yes. You don't think we're going to let on we haven't been up to our necks today, do you? Two highly trained specialists like us?"

Sue sounded so belligerent that Jo laughed aloud at her inconsistency.

"You'll never be able to resist making a good story out of it, Susie. I can just hear the take-off Sergeant Langtree is going to get tonight. And me, too, I fear, for losing my nerve at the very threshold of the signal office. I know you. I guess plenty of the others had the same experience, so we should worry. Give the lads time and they'll be hollering for us instead of wondering what in the devil to do with us now they have us—I hope."

As they rounded the far edge of the parade ground, the early-evening quiet was broken by a round clear trumpet call sounding "Retreat."

At the first note of the service call Jo and Sue came quietly to attention facing the flagstaff at the other end of the field. With their eyes fixed on the emblem of their country,

The WAC checkers player hesitates. . . . It looks as if the staff sergeant has the edge in this off-duty game in the Service Club at Stewart Field, New York.

whose colors seemed to deepen and glow as the lengthening rays of the spring sun lingered on them, they experienced the familiar quickening of pulse that had become an active manifestation in paying honor to their flag—a manifestation that never lessened with repetition.

As the last note of the trumpet died away, the evening gun was fired to symbolize the close of routine activities for the day. Again the trumpet call poured over the wide reaches of the huge base—sounding "To the Color" instead of the National Anthem, which was usually played by the post band. At the first note the girls gave the hand salute and held it until the last note of the call. Although their eyes never wavered from the flagstaff from which the colors were being lowered, they were conscious of the sudden quiet and cessation of movement throughout the wide area of the post. At the first sound of "Retreat" all vehicles in motion had been brought to a halt as for a brief instant in the busy day the entire military personnel paused to render homage to the nation's flag.

A grinding of gears and the snort of a motorcycle broke the spell as the girls turned toward their barracks.

"I get goose pimples every time I stand Retreat," said Sue, with a little shiver. "I'll probably have 'em in layers next Sunday when we have our first formal retreat parade. Even as a civilian, a military band and a color guard gave me shivers along my spine and tears in my eyes. I still get them, but somehow it's a lot more personal now."

"I know how you feel—protective and humble and full of pride all at the same time. The sight of the flag always has given me a very special thrill, ever since I can remember; but it was an involuntary kind of response that I had. Every time I salute it, as we did just now, I find myself making a promise that I'll do anything, all my life, to help make that red-white-and-blue stand for a country that wants freedom for everybody, all over the world—not just for me and my folks and my America."

Sue stole a look at Jo's face as they turned into the path leading to their own area. At the same moment Jo's stern expression relaxed and she looked down at her friend—who was shorter by almost a head—with a wholly natural smile.

"Sounded kind of pompous, didn't I?"

"No," said Sue simply. "I feel the same way—only I'm too darned inarticulate to express it. Anyhow, I feel bucked up a little about being a glorified Western Union girl; and if the Air Forces really need me to run errands, I'll run 'em. Just listen to who's talking, will you? After all, I've got to set a good example to my squad! If the CO didn't treat us all like a bunch of children and try to wipe everybody's individual nose, I might remember my two little stripes more often. Why doesn't she tell us noncoms when she doesn't like the way Auxiliary So'n'so wears her galoshes? Heck, I'll bet Lieutenant Nolan and Sergeant O'Connell know the name of every gal in the whole company by this time, while the CO has to think fast to remember us noncoms."

"That's not fair, Susie. Just think of the million and one other details she has to worry about. Meanwhile it's up to you and me to help make our barracks the best darn outfit in the company. That's part of our job, not the CO's. Right?"

"O.K., Josie. It certainly isn't her fault that our 'bright, blue yonder' looks yonderer than we expected, and blue but not particularly bright."

"You make up the craziest words—'yonderer.' You must have a revolving jaw to get around that one."

Jo smiled at Sue's suddenly cheerful expression as they entered their barracks.

"Do you know what?"

"No. What?"

87

The familiar question, which had become a habit with the Three B's before making an announcement of intention or proposal to one another, made Jo pause at the door of Sue's room and look expectantly at her friend.

"I feel like a million dollars all of a sudden."

"I do, too, Susie. Bring on tomorrow. I'm ready for it now—and for yonder, unlimited."

"Sufficient unto tomorrow is the evil thereof," misquoted Sue jauntily. "I'm ready for chow, unlimited, but immediately."

No explanation was needed between them for their sudden change of mood. They were good enough friends to know that they were over the bump of self-pity, for the time being at least, and better prepared to meet all the tomorrows that lay ahead.

CHAPTER VII

Ladies in the Dark

It had been a busy evening in the orderly room. It seemed to Jo, as she finished taking down the last bed-check report from the barracks police over the telephone, that there had never been so many absentees who had to be accounted for before she could turn in for a nap. From 5:30 P.M., when she had gone on duty in charge of quarters, there had been a constant stream of telephone calls—a threatened case of appendicitis that meant calling an ambulance from the station hospital, long-distance messages to be relayed to wives and sweethearts in every part of the area, even an anxious soldier who wanted her opinion as to whether there was a possibility of Auxiliary Murphy's getting a three-day pass two weeks hence. Her arm ached from holding the receiver to her ear for long stretches.

Also there had been a mixup over a pass that the first sergeant had handed her in the middle of a telephone call. It had been signed by the CO, but the name had not been filled in and Jo could not remember for the life of her whether Sergeant O'Connell had said it was for Brown or Breckenridge. Brown had appeared and asked for her pass; so Jo had filled in her name, hoping that Breckenridge wouldn't show up on the same errand. But she had appeared, and what a time the poor CQ had straightening out that tangle! By the time the indignant Breckenridge had departed, delayed and fuming, Jo's good nature and tact had been stretched to the snapping point.

With a sigh she looked over the long list reported by the BP's as missing at bed check. It was nearly as long as her arm and had to be checked against the cards that were kept in the orderly room—cards of those members who were off the base on pass, in hospital, on emergency duty. A good two or three hours' work were before her.

By midnight the telephone had stopped its persistent ringing and by two o'clock her work was finished, with the cards of those still out on late pass laid out for their owners when they signed in.

Stifling a yawn, Jo called the operator and asked to be called at six o'clock—when she had to wake the mess officer and sergeant. She knew from experience that a knock on Lieutenant Nolan's door sufficed, but Sergeant Kemple was another matter. In response to a sharp rapping on her door there would be a groan, then a mutter, and Sergeant Kemple would be sound asleep again. Next the CQ would have to enter the room boldly, shake the sleeper vigorously by the shoulder or whatever portion of her muffled form she could seize upon, while pleading with her in ever-increasing anxiety to wake up. Not until the good sergeant was upright could Jo be sure that this particular duty had been discharged. By that time she herself would be wide awake and with plenty to do before going off duty at seven-thirty.

Half asleep, she spread the hard cot with her own bedding, draped her uniform over a chair, and by the time she was under the covers she was lost to the world.

The cot—which Sue had dubbed "Bouncing Bet" because it was like a gamble that didn't pay off—had never seemed so soft and welcome, but her head had hardly touched the pillow, or so it seemed, when Jo began to be dimly conscious that something was wrong somewhere. Surely she

90

When the war is over this WAC airplane mechanic won't-need to sit helpless by the side of the road if her automobile gets a cranky streak.

hadn't slept through her six-o'clock telephone call, she thought, groping for her flashlight beneath the bed so she could check the time by her watch. For a moment she lay on her face so drugged with sleep that her hand touching the flashlight seemed powerless to close over it.

Down the corridor from the orderly room a door was wrenched open and Sergeant Kemple's strong voice echoed through the building.

"My gosh, I didn't wake Kemple!"

Conscience-stricken, Jo had flung back the covers and shoved her feet into her waiting oxfords before she became really aware of the sound that had wakened her—a shrill sustained blast like a terrifically loud automobile horn that has started to blow and can't be shut off. By the time she had flung on her bathrobe and reached the door of the orderly room she saw Sergeant Kemple dash from the building buttoning up her uniform blouse as she tore out of the door.

Over her shoulder she flung the words "It's an alert! We've got to get those women out of bed and to their posts and tell 'em not to forget their gas masks."

Jo glanced at her watch—it was just four o'clock and dark as the middle of the night.

A few nights before, in company meeting, the detachment had been instructed in the details of procedure during an alert. Every member had been assigned to a certain area on the base, whither she was to report posthaste—complete with gas mask. Beyond making sure that she knew the location of her area, no one had given the matter much thought, since they had so recently arrived on the base. Never having heard the sound of the alert signal itself, most of the girls, like Jo, thought it was a fire whistle if they woke up at all. Almost no one identified it as an alert at any rate, and for a few moments confusion was rife throughout the whole area.

Since she was CQ, Jo had to remain on duty in the

These Stewart Field (N. Y.) WAC's are learning to become engineering clerks. Working in the buildings along the hangar line they will keep the flying time of engines, record repairs and in general do the paperwork that keeps Army Air Forces plane engines in A-1 shape. These WAC's have previously taken an airplane mechanic's course.

orderly room; but as she watched the exodus of sleep-bewildered WAACs headed toward their various posts on the run, she couldn't restrain the laughter that left her all but helpless.

Spurred on by the mess sergeant's agonized pleas to get going and the first sergeant's brusque orders to put their overcoats over their blue pajamas and their fatigue hats on their heads, to wear oxfords not bedroom slippers, and to be sure to take their gas masks, the detachment dashed out into the bleak darkness.

Pajama legs stuck out below OD topcoats, and Jo heard Captain Cramer's anxious commands to more than one bewildered sleepwalker—"Roll up your legs, for mercy's sake."

Shaking hands struggled with the gas mask carrier straps. Wisps of hair and curlers of all descriptions peeked out from under the floppy brims of fatigue hats, and shoe-laces were tied in such a variety of knots that their owners could hardly get them undone when they finally returned to their barracks.

In the midst of this sudden madhouse performance Jo tried to be reassuring as she helped to adjust straps and belts and speed the stragglers on their way.

Captain Cramer, fully dressed and calm in spite of what Jo knew must be real agony of mind at seeing the members of her company running around like a flock of distracted hens, did her best to bring order out of chaos, but she couldn't be everywhere at once.

"For goodness sake, put on your oxfords instead of those tennis shoes," Jo heard her say to one girl, who looked almost jaunty with her hat riding high over a mass of bobby pins.

"But, ma'am—my oxfords hurt my feet," and the white canvas shoes twinkled off into the blackness with their wearer clutching her hat to her head with one hand while the other

WAC's have shown that an aptitude for mechanics is very strong in some women. Repair jobs are dirty but fascinating work and this WAC looks as if she were far beyond the "hairpin-fixit" stage.

kept reaching desperately for a refractory pajama leg that kept sliding down below the hem of her overcoat.

With an almost audible groan Captain Cramer watched her charges depart, a motley crew of scurrying figures—limping, leaping, scrambling toward their assigned posts, unconscious of their commander's anguish. Intent only upon carrying out orders to the best of their ability, they were mercifully too concerned with finding their way in the dark over still unfamiliar territory to realize, for the moment, that male eyes might be fixed in consternation upon intimate items such as curl papers and escaping pajama legs.

By the time most of the girls had arrived at their destinations, however, the hats had been screwed down to the eyebrow line in cases where camouflage was necessary, and few glimpses of blue showed beneath the hem of buttoned-up overcoats. The new gas masks, however, hung at all angles from belts or shoulders, for no one apparently had expected an air-raid drill during their first ten days after arrival.

The thought that it might be the real thing instead of a drill was sobering to the girls as they awaited instructions to carry out their duties in evacuating the officers' wives and children from the quarters where they were stationed. Trucks assigned for evacuation rolled up in the darkness, but no orders came to fill them; so gradually the tension lessened. By the time the "All Clear" signal was given, a feeling almost of disappointment replaced the nervous dread with which the rudely awakened company had dashed out to perform a hazily conceived responsibility.

No time was lost, however, in the return to barracks. While everyone felt pretty sheepish about having been caught unawares, the girls felt that, though their appearance was decidedly informal, their efforts en route had prevented them from being comical in the eyes of the soldiers on duty. As they filed past Sergeant O'Connell and Captain Cramer upon entering their own area, they were relieved to be greeted by a smile on their CO's face and a heartening grin from the first sergeant.

"We've got to hurry up that requisition for coveralls, Sergeant," said Captain Cramer when the last unit had marched smartly past.

"Yes, ma'am."

A slight emphasis on the second word was the only comment the sergeant allowed herself to indicate her relief that this ordeal was over, but the corners of her mouth twitched as she saluted and stepped back a pace to allow the officer to precede her into the orderly room.

At the entrance Captain Cramer paused and swung to face her right-hand bower.

"And, Sergeant . . . "

The officer's voice was hardly more than a whisper, but it held such a note of rueful laughter that Sergeant O'Connell's "Yes, ma'am?" had a large question mark at the end of it.

"Remind me to wear my gas mask next time, will you?"

"Yes, ma'am," and, as she held the door open for the CO, the sergeant made no attempt to hide her wide grin of appreciation. "We'll do it up in style next time, ma'am," she promised, "in zoot suits."

CHAPTER VIII

Blind Flight

After that first afternoon when Angela and the three "sons" had won over Sergeant Dan Martin and the few men still left in the base photo lab—by the cheerful spirit in which they tackled menial tasks—their training began in earnest. As the weeks passed, even Lieutenant Cooper began to view the results of a day's work with considerable satisfaction.

Meeting Lieutenant Nolan one day in the PX, he drew her aside and looked down at her with a twinkle that even his spectacles couldn't hide.

"Now look here," began Ruth Nolan, who had endured with admirable restraint the lieutenant's anecdotes about his "butter brains," as he called his four new workers.

Privately she had decided that the gleam in his eye and the enthusiasm with which he related misadventures in the laboratory belied his words of disparagement.

Lieutenant Cooper silenced her with an upraised hand.

"Take it easy, you old fire-eater. That red hair of yours is going to get you in trouble one of these days. It's my favorite color, red."

"My friends call it auburn," said Ruth calmly. "What's on your mind? It better be good. I'm too busy to listen to your tale of woe today."

"But that's just the point, Ruth. I've lost my tale of woe. I've just come back, you know, from quite a swing around

WAC's are also airplane mechanics, as are these two shown here working on a plane motor. With no previous experience, WAC's are trained to repair and assist in overhauling the big plane motors.

several other airfields and I've decided I wouldn't change my four WAACs for any in the Air Forces! They're good; in fact, they're colossal! Yeah, I know I called 'em dead ducks; but I've changed my mind. That little Angela has the makings of an ace photographer, and as for Johnson, Matson, and Hanson—well, we're turning out the stuff, and I thought it was only fair to tell you so. Pretty noble of me, after all my hollering, don't you think?"

"You'd be a skunk if you didn't admit it," began Ruth indignantly, but the lieutenant again stopped her with an imperative gesture.

"This is my speech," he insisted. "All right, so you told me in the beginning I'd eat my words. O.K., I've eaten them —some of them anyhow. Aren't you pleased and surprised?"

"Pleased that you've eaten them but not surprised that you had cause to. I hope you'll remember to tell Captain Cramer that the WAACs have actually succeeded in pleasing your lordship."

"Of course they're far from being experts—" began the lieutenant hastily.

"What do you expect in six weeks? You're a perfectionist—that's your trouble."

"You make it sound like a disease."

Lieutenant Cooper sounded so reproachful that Ruth laughed and assured him that she hadn't meant the word as an insult.

"And, at the risk of getting you all puffed up, I'll even add that your four WAACs think you're tops. Apparently they want to be perfectionists, too, just like Papa. Even those hours of nightwork you hang on them don't seem to phase them. But don't push them too hard. They're human, even if you aren't—when it comes to work, I mean."

"Good thing you added that, my auburn-haired mentor. I hear you're a regular slave driver yourself, as all good mess officers—and photographers—have to be. Speaking of being human, or did my ears deceive me, how about tripping the light fantastic with me at the next Officers' Club dance?"

"Don't tell me you ever leave your smelly old darkroom long enough to attend a dance?"

Ruth's eyes grew round with pretended amazement.

"Tsch, tsch," reproved the lieutenant. "Laboratory, not darkroom. It isn't smelly and I am a very nifty tripper, if I do say so. How about it?"

"I'll try anything once," agreed Ruth, with a humorous shrug. "But I'll have to see it to believe it," she added bluntly.

Meanwhile Jo and Sue were far from experiencing the satisfaction that the other member of the Three B's was having in her work.

After almost two weeks of duty in the signal office, where they continued to feel that they were nothing but "glorified Western Union messengers," they seized an unexpected opportunity to do something about their situation.

One morning when they were alone in the office Major Crandall, who had welcomed them cordially on their first day and then apparently dismissed them from his mind, appeared in the doorway and stood with his hands clasped behind his back, regarding them with fatherly interest.

"And how are things going with you?" he asked.

He seemed so approachable and informal in his manner that, without plan or intention, both girls found themselves telling him quite naturally and frankly that from their point of view things weren't going at all—just standing still.

"After all, sir," said Sue impulsively, "we went through three months of specialized training. We're radio mechanics, or supposed to be, sir."

"There just isn't enough work here to keep us busy, sir,"

101

added Jo, completely forgetting for the moment all the instructions they had had about "channeling" procedures.

"Radios, h'm?"

The major raised his grizzled eyebrows quizzically as he looked from one eager girl to the other.

"So it's radios you want," he repeated, pinching his ear thoughtfully. "Well, I guess we ought to be able to fix that for you all right."

When he had gone the two girls looked at each other triumphantly for a moment until it began to dawn on them what they had done.

"Channels!" gasped Jo at length.

Sue nodded gloomily.

"You said it. But I couldn't help it. He was so friendly —it was just like telling my own Dad all about it, instead of asking the first sergeant for permission to talk to the CO, and the CO to talk to somebody else, and somebody else to tell the major we wanted to keep busy."

"Maybe he forgot about channeling too. At any rate he didn't seem to mind, and he did promise to do something about it."

For a day or two they were in a state of suspense, wondering whether they would be called to account for having failed to channel their request properly, but since no message was received to report to the orderly room they began to breathe easier.

On the third day after the major's visit Sergeant Langtree informed them that they were to report the next day to Storeroom K in the basement of the building.

"You'd better come in your coveralls," he advised them, with a slow grin.

Storeroom K proved to be a great barn of a place that seemed filled to the brim with castoff radio sets of every size and description. Their job, along with several enlisted men,

Jeeps, planes, and pilots are part of the everyday job to a WAC in the operations division of an air base.

was to dismantle these sets, salvaging all possible parts that could be used again. It was dirty, often backbreaking work, but Sue and Jo set to with energy and sacrificed fingernails gladly in the good of the cause.

At the end of six weeks the sets had been reduced to neat assortments of usable parts. The wreckage of battered cases and useless odds and ends had been disposed of and Storeroom K was hardly recognizable as the dump heap it had seemed on the first day the girls had begun to work in it.

"Maybe we ought to start channeling again," said Sue, looking around the room with considerable satisfaction. "It doesn't look as if there was much more to be done in this black hole of Calcutta."

"*Again?*"

Jo stressed the word as if to remind Sue of the informal manner in which they had secured a change in their work.

"Speaking of same—don't look now, but here comes the major. Funny how he seems to turn up at the psychological moments in our lives."

Major Crandall strolled around the storeroom for a few moments and came to a halt beside the two begrimed coveralled figures.

"I told you I'd find radios for you, didn't I?" he said, looking very pleased with himself.

"You did indeed, sir," agreed Sue, very conscious of a smudge on her nose that she could see out of the corner of her eye.

"And what would you like to do next, may I ask?"

The question was shot at them so unexpectedly that the girls could only stare at the major speechlessly.

"Well, speak up. You seem to have run out of material on this job, you know."

The major's voice was gruff, but his deep-set eyes had laughter wrinkles at the corners.

But this time they held back the impulse to disregard proper procedures by making any specific requests.

"Anything at all, sir, just so it's a job that is really needed," Jo managed at last.

"H'm. Well, we'll think it over and let you know. I like your spirit."

With a slow nod of his big grizzled head the major pushed his lips in and out as he looked around the orderly workroom.

The girls could hardly wait until he was out of sight to exchange a congratulatory handshake.

"Wait till Angel hears this one," said Sue, scrubbing at her face preparatory to the long walk back to their own area.

"What one? For all we know we may be headed for another storeroom full of junk."

"Not if I know the major. He knows two good radio mechanics when he sees them, I betcha."

At least he knew two intelligent WAACs when he saw them—as they were to discover a day or so later, when they were summoned to Captain Cramer's office for separate interviews.

Sue's appointment followed Josephine's immediately, so there was no opportunity to ask for news. She rolled her eyes comically when she saw Jo leave the captain's office, swallowed hard to down her nervousness, removed her hat and smoothed her hair before knocking on the door beyond which she must face the officer toward whom she had directed such outspoken criticism.

At Captain Cramer's cheerful invitation to enter, Sue marched smartly up to within three paces of the desk, halted, saluted, and reported with approved formality.

"Corporal Bates reporting to the Commanding Officer as ordered."

An hour later she burst into Jo's room, stuttering with excitement.

"What a day! What a CO! What a perfectly humdingnaceous assignment! Josie, I'm reporting to the traffic office tomorrow and Captain Cramer says there's a bare possibility that there'll be an opportunity to get into the control tower later on. Oh, boy! Oh, boy! Oh, boy! Am I crazy or am I crazy?"

Sue spun around in the narrow room like a top before flinging herself beside Jo on the bed.

"I hoped maybe she'd tell me where you were going, but she didn't. All she said was that she expected to be very proud of the Three B's before the year was over. Imagine! She actually called us that, and looked as pleased as I felt. You're right, as usual, Josie. She's swell."

"And so is our good friend the major. Don't forget him. Guess what?"

"You're going to traffic, too! But, no—that would be too perfect."

"You'd never guess, and I'm scared green but tickled pink. I'm going into the instrument flying section, and if I make good I'll be a Link Trainer Instructor in time. And no cracks, please, about Missing Links."

Jo held up the book she had been reading when Sue burst in upon her.

"I went over to the library while you were with the CO and hunted up this treatise on *Blind Flight*. I can't make head or tail of it so far, but trying to will be a lovely way to spend the evening."

"You'll spend no evening with no book," said Sue, taking the slim volume from Jo's hands and planking it firmly down upon the small bookcase at the head of the bed. "You haven't forgotten you promised to go to Squadron B's farewell party tonight with Johnny and me, I hope. We've got to

106

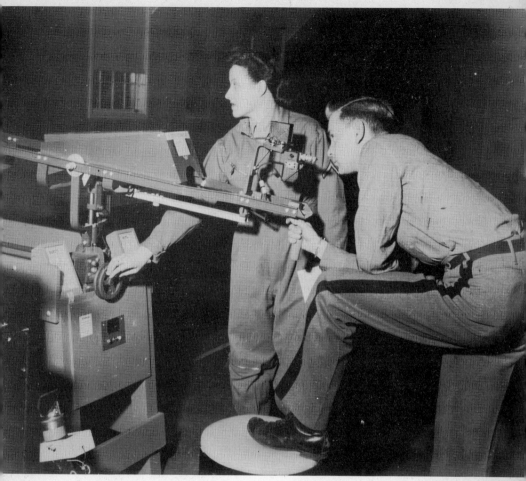

On this device the West Point cadet pictured learns his gunnery. The WAC instructor at Stewart Field—"the Wings of West Point"—sets the machine preparatory to the cadet's letting go a "burst" at a model plane. The WAC is assigned to the Training Aids section of the field.

celebrate this occasion, believe me. Besides, Johnny's wearing his corporal's stripes for the first time and he'd be crushed not to have an admiring audience."

"But, Sue—" began Jo.

Sue whirled on her and shook a finger warningly under her nose.

"But me no buts. You promised. So did Angel, and then she goes and lets old Dragon-Eye put her on emergency duty in the photo lab tonight."

"You don't suppose she had any choice in the matter, do you?"

"Maybe yes, maybe no. I hope I'm wrong, but this war may last for years and years."

Sue sounded so concerned that Jo looked at her curiously.

"What in the world are you talking about? I don't see what the length of the war has to do with Angel's not going to Squadron B's party tonight. She has to work—what's so disturbing about that?"

Instead of answering immediately, Sue studied an enlarged snapshot of Lieutenant Bill Garland that stood on top of the bookcase.

"You're lucky," she said finally. "And so is Bill. This crazy business of rank doesn't bother you prewar specimens. But did you ever stop to think how difficult it might be if you had met him *after* you joined the Corps—I mean if you weren't an officer and he was?"

"I can't say I've lost any sleep over it. I've known Bill ever since I was in the sixth grade. I don't expect to be in the Army all my life and neither does Bill. I'm quite sure he doesn't care whether I'm a corporal or a captain."

"He might care if you *were* a captain. Look at Johnny. He's never said much, but it sure has griped him to have me outrank him. I hope I don't beat him to three stripes. I'm afraid it would be the end of a beautiful friendship. Sometimes this whole business of rank seems so unreal. Regulations and unwritten laws can't keep people from falling in love, even if they can make it darned uncomfortable for them."

"If you are worrying about Angel and Lieutenant Cooper, forget it. She has her heart set on being sent overseas and she's working like fury to learn enough to be ready if the opportunity comes. The trouble with you is that you can't imagine anyone being so interested in a job that it means more than having dates."

"Oh, nuts! When that happens there's more than love for the job involved. A fine pair of friends I picked out, I must say. Are you going to Squadron B with me or not? We'll have to step on it. Johnny said he'd meet us in the dayroom at seven sharp."

"O.K. I'll be ready by the time you are."

As she changed into her freshly pressed best uniform, Jo tried to emulate the gaiety with which Sue flung herself into any social occasion. For a full minute she regarded her severe expression in her hand mirror until a mocking smile lifted the corners of her mouth.

"I'll probably have a wonderful time, once I get there," she thought. "I usually do when it's as hard to get going as this. Sue's right—I mustn't be a stick in the mud."

With firm fingers she moved Bill's picture to her side of the bookcase and snapped off the light, still seeing his face plain before her—more real, for a·moment, than the hard surface of the doorknob under her hand.

The party in Squadron B's mess hall turned out to be a very lively, noisy affair and for a while Jo did not have to make any effort to enjoy herself. It had been a long tiring day, however, and she began to wish she could think up a good excuse to leave without Sue's being aware of it.

At the far end of the mess hall, which had been cleared of its tables to make room for informal dancing, she could see a solitary cook busily frying doughnuts for the crowd. She wandered into the spotless kitchen and stood slightly behind him watching his skillful manipulation of batter and bubbling fat. Without taking his eyes from the deep iron kettle and its sizzling contents, the cook suddenly reached for a second pot of fat, at the far end of the range, that was melted but fortunately not boiling. Just as his hand seized the handle his foot slipped, causing him to bear down on the pot handle with such force that the heated grease rose like a water spout toward Jo, hit her full force on the front of her uniform from collar to hem, and dribbled down onto her stockings and oxfords in a spreading stain.

"Oh, migosh! Oh, migosh!" moaned the young soldier, a look of agonized self-reproach on his freckled face.

"Don't mind me. Your doughnuts are burning."

Jo pointed to the bubbling kettle, from which a wreath of bluish haze was beginning to rise.

"Oh, migosh!" yelped the cook even more shrilly.

Skidding over the greasy floor, he began to scoop the dark brown batch into a wire strainer—hopping from side to side as if the floor were burning the soles of his feet.

Not until the doughnuts were safely removed and a new batch beginning to swell and bob about on the surface of the fat did he turn again to Jo, who was calmly blowing on one of the crisp dark brown circles until it should be cool enough to eat.

"You might as well let me help you finish the job," she said, with a grin. "No more dancing for me tonight."

"Gee whiz, ma'am—I mean Corporal. I don't know how

that happened, honest I don't. Oh, migosh! Just look at your uniform. I'll have it cleaned for you."

"Nonsense! It wasn't your fault. Anyhow, I was just wondering what excuse I could have for getting back home before the party was over. I've got a good one now, but I'd rather fry doughnuts. Come on; let's heat up the second kettle of fat—what's left of it—and I'll help you turn these out in double-quick time."

"I'll get you an apron," began the cook, and then stopped with a comically horrified look at Jo's ruined clothes.

"Turn 'em over," commanded Jo, pointing at the kettle, and grinned again when the soldier obeyed with alacrity.

By the time the last batch was finished Jo knew she had made a good friend of Sandy Thomas.

"I still feel terrible about having this happen to you," he said as he handed her her hat and shoulder bag, which he had rescued from the other end of the mess hall so she could slip out of the back door. "I bet I get hell from the mess sergeant."

"How's he going to know about it? We cleaned everything up, didn't we? And nobody's going to see me—you can bet on that. I had a swell time, Sandy; really I did. I'm sorry you're leaving so soon, but I guess you aren't."

"But I'm not leaving—that's the heck of it."

Sandy looked so forlorn that Jo was sorry she had mentioned the Squadron's departure.

"Well, you can't blame us for hanging on to a doughnut expert when we get one, can you? The next time we put on a dance, why don't you come over to see us?"

"Gosh, I don't know any girls on this field. In fact, I just about won't know anyone here when our fellows pull out."

"You know me, don't you? I'll send you a special invitation and see that you do meet some girls. We've got plenty."

111

"Well—" Sandy fidgeted uneasily for a moment, swallowed with apparent effort, and blurted out a question that seemed to surprise him almost as much as it did Jo. "I don't suppose you'd go to the movies with me Saturday night, would you? I'd kind of like to do something to make up for that shower bath I gave you tonight."

"Why, sure, I'd like to. I'll meet you in our dayroom."

"That's sure swell of you. I've never been over to that date bazaar of yours, so I sure hope you don't stand me up."

Sandy's look of anxiety was replaced by such a beam of pleasure that Jo was thankful she hadn't hesitated to accept his invitation.

"I'll be there, with a doughnut in my buttonhole in case you've forgotten what I look like."

"Don't remind me of them, please. Still, I wouldn't ever have had the nerve to ask you if it hadn't been for that pot of grease. I'm just a private first class, you know. Do you mind?"

"Good heavens, what difference does that make?"

Jo sounded so sincerely impatient over the idea of one stripe more or less that Sandy grinned happily.

"I'll tell your friend you had a telephone call or something," he promised as he stepped out of doors to point out a short cut to the WAAC area. "Oh, migosh! It's raining! Wait a minute and I'll grab a raincoat for you."

"Don't bother, please. I'm practically wearing oilskins, remember? The rain will run off me like water from a duck's back."

As she rounded the corner of the brightly lighted mess hall she turned to wave at Sandy, who she felt was still looking after her.

"Saturday night, remember," he shouted cheerfully as she disappeared into the darkness.

The rain was falling heavily before she reached her barracks, but in spite of her soggy, grease-stiffened garments she felt strangely lighthearted.

Once in her bare room, she stripped off her clothes and regarded her ruined oxfords. The uniform could be cleaned, but she knew those shoes were done for.

"I ought to feel like the hole in one of Sandy's doughnuts, but I don't," she thought as she picked up the incomprehensible volume she had been reading earlier in the evening.

The barracks were apparently deserted, for an unusual peace and quiet reigned. At length, however, Jo had to admit that she knew little more than when she began to read.

"*Blind Flight*," she murmured as she laid the book away. "I don't like that name. It fits what I've been doing these past months too well. I'm glad the name of my new section is Instrument Flying Department. It has a good, solid, dependable sound."

She studied Bill's face for a moment before she turned out the light.

"And you have a good, solid, dependable look, young feller. Just don't forget to fly back home again—that's all. And not by the seat of your pants, please. I'd like you back all in one piece, if possible."

The thought of having an opportunity to help other young pilots to a surer chance of flying back home again was a very comforting one as Jo faced tomorrow with more anticipation than she had known for many weeks.

CHAPTER IX

Link Trainers

As Jo entered the door of the long low wooden structure inconspicuously labeled "Instrument Flying Department," she showed none of the shyness that had come upon her the morning she and Sue had reported for duty on their first assignment at the air base. She had often looked at this particular building in passing with a certain amount of curiosity, never dreaming that she was soon to be initiated into the mysteries of the Link trainer.

Unlike Sue, who was more or less content to take every day as it came, absorbing information and experience on the job and in training sessions, Jo had set out to learn all she could about the development of air power, through long hours of reading at the library or from questioning the men with whom she worked. Like so many young people of her age, she had long been fascinated by the subject of airplanes and had dreamed of being a flyer herself until the United States had been drawn into the war. With her brother she had learned to make exact models of aircraft that were used in Army training centers in teaching plane identification. A preflight course in college had been an absorbing experience to her and, while she had had no actual experience in flying a plane, she was familiar with the principles of flight and the operation of a plane.

It was with especial anticipation, therefore, that she

114

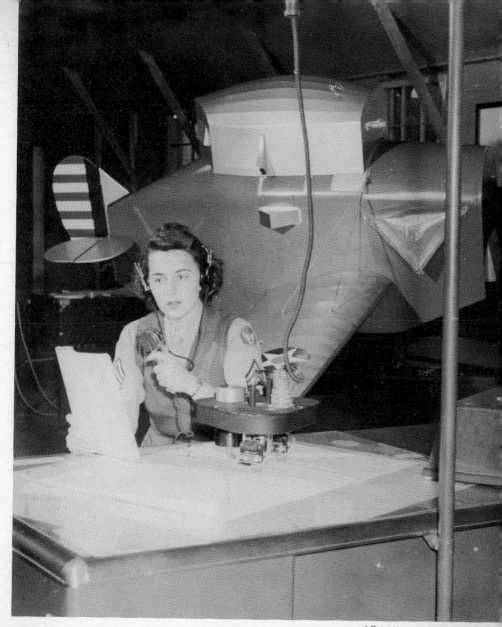

Official U. S. AAF photo

The Link trainer is an earth-bound "plane" in which the pilot flies "blind." All his maneuvers are recorded at an instrument desk manned by a Link trainer instructor. A number of WAC's have qualified for this highly technical instruction.

began her first day on her new job, for she had the double satisfaction of looking forward to learning more about a subject in which she was deeply interested while releasing a man for active service.

She had never been in the instrument flying department before, so she looked about her with keen interest. The effect of the long, rather narrow room that housed a row of Link trainers was wholly pleasant. Windows on both sides of the building gave the room a cheerful, bright appearance that was enhanced by the spotless condition of the concrete floor painted gray and the brightly colored trainers that seemed poised for flight. Their bodies were painted a bright lively blue, their stubby wings a brilliant yellow or silver, and some of their perky rudders were gaily striped with red and white.

A few feet behind each trainer was placed an instructor's table on which rested a triangular instrument mounted on wheels that recorded, on a chart spread over the top of the instructor's desk, the details of the flight made by pilots within the trainer.

A voice from the far end of the room broke in upon Jo's absorbed observation of her new place of work, and she peered around the end of the trainer that she had been inspecting to find three pairs of eyes regarding her from the floor beneath the furthermost trainer.

A round-faced sergeant, squatting on his heels beside the black box from which two men—one of them flat on his back —were removing the turbine that operated the trainer, grinned up at her as she approached and waved a welcome.

"Be with you in a moment. You can put your things in the office down below there."

The other two men didn't even look up from their work, so Jo wandered down to the small cluttered room at the end of the training section and hung her hat and shoulder bag on a nondescript coat rack in a corner. The walls of the office were covered with highly colored photographs of ships of all descriptions and as she turned to study the nearest set she was startled by a scratching sound followed by a small comical yawn that ended in an urgent whimper. In a rude crate padded with waste she discovered a tiny, fuzzy-haired black and brown Airedale puppy begging so beseechingly for attention that she lifted him from his bed and cuddled his wriggling ecstatic form in her arms.

He responded to her murmured reassurances with tiny yelps of delight and began gnawing at her fingers with such eagerness that she wondered whether he had had any breakfast. Her experience with her own brothers had convinced her that boys could be very casual about looking after the practical needs of their pets. In spite of the fact that it was she rather than they who saw the succession of small animals through the trials of infancy, the little beasts invariably gave their harum-scarum masters the full measure of their devotion. Remembering the times without number when she had acted as nursemaid, trainer, and provider in the past, Jo was about to replace the small wriggler, who was already insinuating himself into her affections, when the round-faced sergeant entered the office, regarding her with a mixture of relief and approval.

"He's hungry," said Jo accusingly as she deposited the protesting ball of fur in his box.

"Sure—he's always hungry. I think one of the fellows gave him some breakfast though."

"Whom does he belong to? I don't think he's being fed properly. He's just skin and bone under that puppy fuzz."

"The little beggar just walked in here the other day when the door was open. We think maybe he belongs to one of the officers' kids, but nobody has claimed him and we couldn't just turn the little beggar out in the cold. How would you like to take him on?"

"I was sent here to learn about Link trainers, not to be a puppy nurse," said Jo, amused by the note of real eagerness in Sergeant Baker's voice. "But I'll keep an eye on him, just in case you boys neglect him. Heaven knows I've had plenty of experience."

"How about flying? Had any experience in that?"

"Very little, and none at all with the kind you teach here —blind flight."

"O.K. We'll start at the bottom. We haven't a heavy schedule today, so come along and we'll put you through the paces."

Sergeant Baker led Jo to one of the trainers in the center of the line and explained its operation while several of the other men gathered round, cracking jokes and offering advice with apparent enjoyment. The novelty of having a woman in the department seemed to strike their sense of humor and that first hour of explanation and instruction was characterized by considerable hilarity at Jo's expense. Her equable disposition and the fact that she had grown up with two brothers made it easy for her to accept both the teasing and the superiority with which they answered her questions and conducted her initiation into the department of instrument flying.

Even Sergeant Baker, who was in charge of the practical work of the department, seemed at first inclined to regard the whole business of having a WAAC assigned to his staff as a rather pleasant but temporary interlude in the day's monotony. His general explanation of the work involved was simple, however, and sincere though casual, and Jo was relieved when he turned her over at last to Corporal Jenson, a shy slender man, older than most of the other members of the group, and told him to take charge of the newcomer's instruction.

Corporal Jenson seemed relieved when the wisecrackers

118

Close-up of a Link trainer, an aviation cadet and a Wac Link trainer instructor. The WAC—who, incidentally, flew in civilian life and held a commercial license—is showing the cadet how his session of instrument flying practice went.

went about their usual duties and he was left alone with Jo in front of an unoccupied trainer that the maintenance crew had just finished servicing.

Disregarding the explanations about the workings of a Link trainer that had been thrown out at random during the past hour, Corporal Jenson began a leisurely description of the development of instrument flying and its importance in the training of pilots. He talked easily, with a faint trace of accent that indicated his Scandinavian origin, and with such genuine enthusiasm for his subject that Jo was increasingly glad to have an opportunity to work with him.

"About the only thing this little gadget can't do is fly upside down," said the corporal, laying a hand almost affectionately on the smooth .enameled surface of the trainer. "Climb in and I'll show you."

The corporal raised the hood of the trainer, exposing the cockpit that was just large enough for one person, and Jo mounted two shallow steps at the side of the trainer and slid into the pilot's seat. The instrument panel in front of her, explained Jenson, had all the essential features of a regular plane and, once he was enclosed in that small space, the pilot was alone with "his memories," his instruments, and the radio by which he was able to receive messages from the ground concerning weather conditions and the beam signal by which he was flying.

The corporal unfastened the strap—a steel bar that held the trainer in a rigid position when it was not in use or until the pilot was in place—and demonstrated the simple principles of contact flying.

"Ever flown a plane?" he asked, seeing how naturally Jo's hands were placed on the stick and her feet on the rudder pedals.

"Not by myself, but I know the principles and have sat

The cockpit of a Link trainer is just large enough to accommodate one person. When the trainer is in actual use, the hood, open in this picture of a WAC instructor at the controls, is closed down.

in the copilot's seat a few times—under the eagle eye of the pilot, of course."

"Good. I'll turn on the juice so you can have the experience at least of trying to keep the bird in level flight. Hope you don't get seasick easily. Want me to put the hood down?"

"Mercy no! I'd be scared pink. Sure I won't bust anything if I start pushing the wrong gadgets?"

"No—just you take it easy until you get the feel of it. Put on your earphones so you can hear my instructions over the radio from the desk. I promise you won't have to worry about turbulent air this trip!"

"Can you really create special weather conditions by pushing those levers on the desk over there?"

"Sure thing. Every once in a while a lazy guy gets in one of these and tries to cheat a little by flying by compass instead of radio beam. When we catch him doing that we shoot him a good little cross wind and the next thing he knows he's thirty or forty miles off course and maybe headed for a mountain peak. All set now—first, you warm up the engine and check the air speed, rate of climb, bank and turn indicator, just as if you were doing a real take-off in a real plane under normal conditions. And if the take-off isn't just right the plane will go into a spin. Of course, if the Link does go into a spin you won't be hurt; but I'll know about it."

The corporal instructed Jo to turn on the ignition switch and she was surprised at the feeling of life that seemed to flow through the trainer. As the Link moved slowly on its pivot, responding with tilted nose and dips to right or left as she handled the controls, her heart quickened its beat. She was glad the hood was open so she could catch a reassuring glimpse of the corporal now and then.

After a few moments of erratic gyrations she called to Jenson and told him she had had enough for the first trial.

From her control desk a WAC Link trainer instructor gives directions to an aviation cadet inside the cockpit of a training device nearby. The cadet, "flying" entirely by instruments, is conducting his "plane" on a hypothetical flight. His progress is recorded on the charts in front of the WAC. Afterwards, the WAC will show the cadet where he made any mistakes.

As he slipped the strap into place and helped her climb down from the Link, she found her knees were shaking.

"That's the eeriest feeling I ever had," she confessed, looking at the now-stationary trainer with something like wonder. "What makes it so—so flexible?"

"Its mobility is largely controlled by a system of bellows. See—" The corporal lifted a black curtain encircling the bottom of the trainer and the black base which supported it. "Pressing the stick to the left compresses one set of bellows and inflates the opposite set, and so on. The small black box in front of the trainer houses the turning motor, which has another intricate set of bellows that you will learn more about when you see the maintenance men overhauling a trainer after every twenty-five hours of flight. Not that you'll have to dirty your hands with that job, but it's interesting to know what makes the wheels go round."

"It all looks very complicated to me right now," Jo admitted after the corporal had seated her at the desk and explained the apparatus used by the instructor in directing the pilot in his enclosed compartment.

Here at least she was on more familiar ground, due to the training she had received at the radio school.

Shortly after she had returned from dinner, refreshed by her long walk to the WAAC area and back, with milk and biscuits secured from the mess hall for Purp's eager consumption, Corporal Jenson explained the details of how a flight plan was made.

"There's a chap over there just starting a problem. Let's look on while he goes over his flight plan with the instructor, and watch him at work. He's a fighter pilot," Jenson added in a low voice, "and not too crazy about having to put in his regular hours of instrument practice. You sure notice a difference in those chaps. They're on their own, pretty much, and some of them think it's a waste of time—all this Link

124

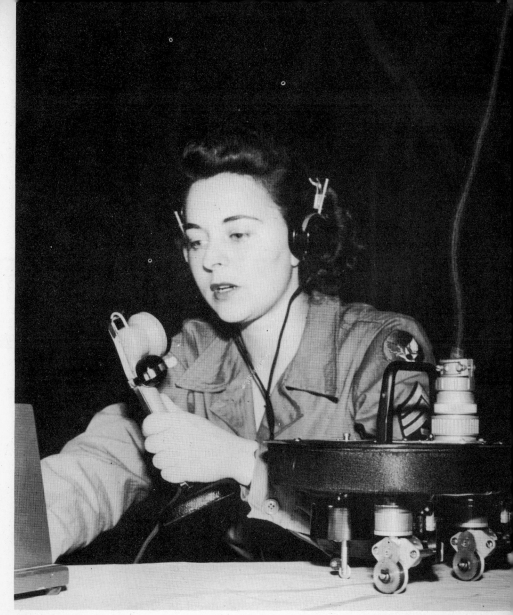

A close-up of a WAC Link trainer instructor at her desk in the Instrument Flying Department. The wheeled instrument at the right records on the chart below it the "flight" of the pilot in the enclosed Link trainer.

trainer business. The bomber pilots usually are very conscientious about it, for so many other lives in addition to their own depend upon them. He's a nice boy, this one, but nine times out of ten the record of one of his Link flights looks like a hare-and-hounds race. He keeps trying though. Mind if we listen in, Lieutenant?"

The stocky blond pilot acknowledged Jo's presence with a broad smile of welcome as he straightened up from the chart which he had been studying with his instructor.

"I've been wondering when you guys were going to raise the level of this hellhole," he said, with a gleam of interest in his bright blue eyes. "How soon will you take me on as a student, Corporal?"

"Well, not for a day or so," Jo replied, smiling at Jenson.

She was aware that the instructor was regarding her somewhat glumly, as if resentful of the interruption. In fact, his annoyance became so marked that she was unable to follow very closely the supplementary information that Jenson conscientiously added from time to time in a low voice.

As the pilot climbed into his trainer and started to lower the hood, he stuck his head out and waved gaily at Jo.

"Be here to welcome me home—mind. But don't watch me fly out of sight—that's bad luck, you know."

Standing beside the instructor's desk with Jenson at her elbow, Jo watched the "take-off"—which was smooth enough as far as she could tell.

From time to time Jenson would shake his head slightly as his eyes followed the recorder that traveled over the chart spread on top of the instructor's desk.

"He'll run out of gas before he gets back to his base, if he doesn't watch out. But he's getting better all the time and I wouldn't be surprised if these hours he spends in the Link may save his skin one of these days."

126

Official U. S. AAF photo

Not a real plane but one of the ingenious devices used by the Training Aids section of Stewart Field, N. Y. to teach West Point cadets some of the elements of flying and shooting without leaving the ground. Specifically, it's the "Gunairstructor," in which the WAC instructor "pilots" an image of an enemy plane on a screen and the cadet in the cockpit behind her attempts to pilot his "plane" into a position to fire. Accompanying this realistic training is the roar of the engines, the rush of the wind and the chatter of machine guns. And when the cadet scores a hit on the enemy plane it flashes red as if bursting into flame.

"I can see why this work is fascinating," Jo said, watching the almost eerie gyrations of the Link as the invisible pilot worked out his flight problem. "The machines and instruments may be perfect and infallible. But the way they perform, after all, depends upon the kind of man at the controls and his handling of them, doesn't it?"

"You're right. If men were all as alike as this row of trainers, our job would become a pretty dull one. There still isn't any machine shop that turns out human nature in one pattern, and I say thank God for it."

Engrossed in watching the progress of the recorder over the white chart, Jo was startled when Sergeant Baker shouted to her from the office that she was to report at once to the dispatcher's office.

Corporal Jenson gave her a pleased grin and urged her to be off in a hurry.

"Looks like you're going to have a trip aloft," he explained. "All Link instructors have them in order to become familiar with actual flying conditions and communications with ground control. That message was from Major Crandall's office. So hop along. Tomorrow we'll tackle the charts and desk instruments with a flight problem. Keep your ears and eyes open now, and we'll make a real instructor of you. I'll tell the lieutenant you couldn't wait to welcome him back from his trip. He'll probably end up on the wrong field anyhow. One time he landed forty feet below ground—on paper."

As Jo hurried on the double-quick toward the hangar line, she had a feeling of being suspended in mid-air. The unexpected summons to the dispatcher's office might prove to be a purely routine matter, in spite of Jenson's interpretation, so she refused to get excited about a possible flight so soon after reporting to duty in the instrument flying department. Besides, her mind was so full of unrelated details

128

regarding her new job that she felt discouraged about ever being able to master even the rudiments of so complicated a procedure. She clutched the booklets Jenson had given her for study and arrived at the operations building feeling almost indifferent over the prospect of a trip aloft.

However, upon being told that Sue had already gone on with Major Crandall and the pilot of a B-17 and she'd better hurry if she was to make the trip with them, she forgot the depressing review that had been running through her mind and ran toward the giant plane to which she had been directed.

CHAPTER X

Traffic Is Terrific

While Jo was being inducted into the intricacies of the
instrument flying department, Sue was feeling very grateful that the ice had already been broken in the traffic office
of the operations building by five other members of the
company, two of whom were now on duty. During the weeks
when she and Jo had been in the signal office, located on the
same corridor of the building, she had often looked in on the
traffic office, wishing that she could be a part of its noisy
bustle of activity. Now that she found herself behind the
long high counter that divided the room into two parts, she
wondered how she would ever have an opportunity to master
what seemed an endless complication of details regarding
maps, charts, teletype messages, weather reports, and the
personalities of pilots and visiting celebrities.

Everyone else behind the counter was so busy that she
had to save up the dozens of questions that came to her mind
until there should be a lull in the activity that stimulated but
bewildered her. She observed with growing respect the two
WAACs who were carrying on their work with enviable
nonchalance and efficiency in the midst of what seemed to
Sue downright turmoil. It was comforting to know that a
few short weeks ago these same two had known the mystifica-
tion and helplessness that she was feeling now. In addition,
they had had to endure the usual trying raised-eyebrows

Official U. S. AAF photo

The air ways of the world—on maps—are familiar territory to WAC's
who work in the operations division of an air base. A new conception of
world neighbors will follow this WAC into civilian life.

period while the men whom they were to replace regarded them with the somewhat bantering skepticism that members of a new detachment of WAACs on a post almost always had to live through.

There were no evidences of this skepticism now as far as Sue could observe, and as the hours passed she could understand why. Her keen eyes missed little as she leaned for the most part against one end of the high counter, careful to get in no one's way and at the same time find many answers to her unasked questions through careful observation.

As she looked on quietly hour after hour, her quick mind seized upon details and stored them away for further pondering and reference. Out of the blur of sound a pattern of meaning began to shape itself.

It was not a large room to house so great an evidence of man's exuberant conquest of the skies. Through the partly opened windows that faced the apron of the main runway came the constant tumult of motors—long, sustained blasts of sound, bursts and snorts of power. A steady far-off hum grew gradually into an immediate thunder as a ship swooped down upon the field, and the roaring challenge with which wide wings left the ground and soared into the sky sent back a diminishing reminder of a vociferous departure. Covering the entire wall behind the counter was a blackboard bulletin of arriving and departing planes. Its two sections, one devoted to transients or visiting ships and the other to ships belonging to the air base, were almost filled with chalked entries that gave the details of arrivals and departures. Round white tags indicated which flights were outgoing; red ones identified planes soon to be expected.

From a loud-speaker high on the wall came a jumble of sound from the control tower that Sue hoped made sense to someone, though as far as she could tell no one paid any

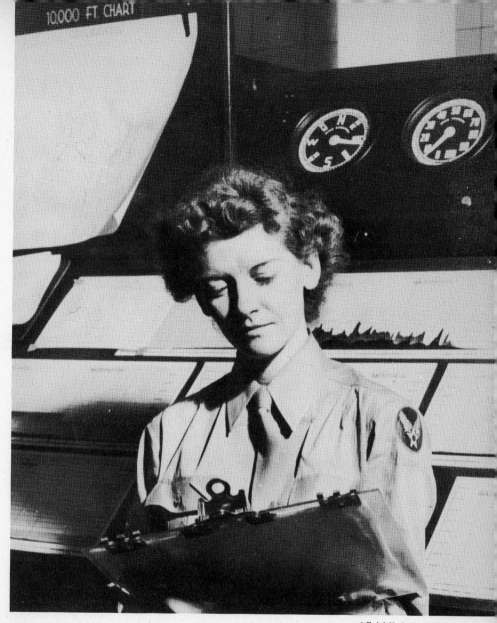

10,000 FT CHART

Without accurate weather information, plane flights would be seriously restricted, so jobs in weather observation are among the most important at an airfield. This WAC is shown compiling a weather chart, used to determine weather conditions in various areas.

attention to the words that might have been Chinese for all the meaning she could make of them.

Through the door that opened onto the runway came pilots with flight plans to be checked and pilots who had just arrived, lugging their parachutes. They brought with them into the congested space an electric element that made Sue's scalp tingle. She looked at them lounging against the counter, exchanging quips with one another, cocky for the most part even when dog-weary from a long flight, and wondered if she would ever be able to work in this surcharged atmosphere with the detached concentration shown by her two coworkers.

She was studying the neat blond head of Private First Class Alice Harrison, who was in the "hot seat"—talking over the telephone and apparently reading messages from the teletype machine, beside her, at the same time. How she could hear anything in the hullabaloo around her Sue couldn't imagine, and yet Alice seemed to think nothing of it as she went over details of the pilot's flight plan before her with the Airways Traffic Control by telephone, checked back with the control tower, and managed to send an occasional smile of greeting to some newcomer who tried to attract her attention over the heads of the men who were lined upon the other side of the counter.

Sue began to appreciate the meaning of the term "hot seat" as she watched Alice at work, and also to be glad that the counter was both a high and a sturdy barrier against the throng that pressed around it.

She was so engrossed in her study of all that was going on around her, in which she hoped soon to be an active part, that she almost jumped when a tall figure leaned across the counter and spoke directly to her.

"Howdy, Corporal. Haven't seen you around here before, have I?"

Giving the go-ahead signal to a Flying Fortress at an Army Air Base, this WAC demonstrates one of the duties performed in a control tower. After surveying conditions on the field, making sure there are no obstacles to a safe takeoff, the WAC squeezes the trigger of the "biscuit gun," flashing a Morse code message to the outgoing aircraft. The control tower operator has to be proficient in handling radio equipment as well as the blinkers.

Sue was on the point of admitting that this was her first day in operations when Major Crandall strolled out of the adjoining weather room, laid a hand on the tall pilot's arm, and asked if he were about ready to take off.

Before turning to answer the major's question the pilot gave Sue a slow wink.

"Any time you say, sir. You're the only passenger, so far."

"H'm," said the major, looking speculatively at Sue, with a twitch of his left eye that she knew indicated inner amusement.

"How about taking a couple of young ladies along, in that case? Sort of give them the feel of what all this hurly-burly is about, eh, Captain?" He turned to Sue with a twinkle in his deep-set eyes. "Just an operational flight—nothing to get excited about. The captain here is a first-class pilot, you know."

The major almost achieved a smile behind his close-clipped mustache at the expression on Sue's face as she looked first at him and then at the pilot. Apparently she wasn't quite sure whether she was being kidded or not.

"I've already sent word to your friend over at the Link section to join us," the major added benevolently. "Come along, Harker. And you too, er, er Corporal—"

"Bates, sir," supplied Sue breathlessly as she dived into a corner for her hat, gloves, and shoulder bag.

It all seemed very informal, she thought as she looked over at Alice Harrison and met the amused eyes of the sergeant in charge of the shift. Alice gave her a wave from the "hot seat," and the sergeant grinned knowingly behind the major's broad back.

Shaking with excitement at the thought of her very first ride in a plane, Sue hurried after the two men wondering what kind of a ship they would be going up in.

Keeping the bulletin board of incoming and outgoing planes up to date is often one of the jobs of a WAC assigned to the traffic office.

The captain led the way to a huge hangar, where he arranged for parachutes and "Mae Wests" for his three passengers. Sue felt very small between the lanky pilot and the broad major; but by the time they had reached the Flying Fortress to which Captain Harker led them she felt more at ease, for its towering bulk dwarfed them in turn.

"So this is the famous *Sally Bee,*" said the major, looking up at the scarred lettering of the plane's name and the yellow jacket in angry flight beside it. "When I remember the old Jenny I used to fly back in 1919—just about the time you were born, young feller—it's hard to believe that General Arnold is already calling your *Sally Bee* the last of the *small* bombers."

The major chuckled when Sue gave an involuntary gasp of amazement.

"If this is a small one you'd like to see a big one, wouldn't you? Well, so would I. And I guess we will before long, eh, Harker?"

"That's right. The B-29 Superfortress makes this old B-17F look like a cub, so they say."

The pilot was stretching out a hand to help Sue climb into the plane behind the major when she saw a figure dash out of the operations building and run toward them.

"Looks as if reinforcements are on the way," he said to Sue, with a wide grin.

Sue looked over her shoulder just as Jo came to a halt beside the tall pilot, breathless from her quick trip over from the Link trainer section.

"Up you go, sister," and with a boost that almost lifted her off her feet Jo was inside the plane, beaming alternately upon Sue and the major.

"I came as fast as I could, sir. I was so afraid you'd go off without me."

"We have time enough. We aren't going far, you know.

Just a short flight to one of the big airplane plants near by, where Captain Harker is going to talk to the workers and let them have a glimpse of one of the big girls who has seen plenty of action. He is going to go all over the country on this kind of job and I thought it was a good opportunity to get a couple of you girls off the ground."

"Goodness, I haven't been *on* the ground for the last fifteen minutes, sir," said Jo fervently. "Pinch me," she added in an undertone to Sue. "Is this us, or am I dreaming? How's traffic?"

Sue grinned as she pinched her own wrist before answering.

"Terrific! And how are all the little Links?"

A sudden roar of sound as the pilot began to warm up the motors drowned Jo's reply. With rounded thumb and forefinger of her right hand she silently answered Sue's question and at the same time set the GI sign of approval on life in general and on this first flight in particular.

CHAPTER XI

"True Faith and Allegiance"

The hot August sun beat mercilessly down on the Three B's as they came out of the mess hall together shortly after noon and made their way to the mailroom at the far end of the headquarters building.

While they waited their turn at the counter they admired the decorations that the mail clerk had put up to mark the historic occasion in which they would soon be participating.

"Maisie never runs out of ideas, does she?" said Sue admiringly as she fingered a cleverly fashioned red, white, and blue rosette on one wall of the small room. From it tiny streamers of crepe paper twirled upwards to mingle in the center of the ceiling with green and yellow strands that led down to a rosette of the same colors on the opposite wall. "I don't particularly care for the combination of colors, but she's captured the significance all right."

The girls nibbled absently on bits of hard candy from a bowl that stood at one end of the counter as they continued to study Maisie Dobson's interpretation of the day's great event—their induction into the Army of the United States as the Women's Army Corps.

"That cherub winging away with the extra A for Auxiliary looks to me like the handiwork of Corporal Borelli," declared Jo, studying a large cutout of Pallas Athena over whose head appeared three freshly gilded letters—"WAC."

This WAC works in the printing department and is shown lifting a roller from a multilith printer. They also operate other types of printing machines, such as the multigraph and mimeograph.

Above the crisp bright legend hovered a mischievous pink and white cherub clasping a single A of somewhat battered appearance.

Angela smilingly admitted that she had made the figure at Maisie's request.

"But she wouldn't tell me what she wanted it for. I thought she was planning to carry out a new joke about being Understudy to Dan Cupid."

Maisie Dobson waved a greeting to the three friends over the heads of the girls crowded in front of the counter and signaled that she had mail for all of them.

"We've been admiring your decorations, Maisie—not that we needed to be reminded what day this is. Somehow I don't feel half so excited now as I did when we used to talk about the possibility of being made a part of the regular Army, way back in basic training. My gosh, we've *been* a part of the Army for almost three months—practically."

"Just wait till you stand up in front of the commandant of the post this afternoon and say 'I do,' and I bet you won't be feeling any too calm. You ought to hear some of the girls who decided not to stay in the Corps. They're the sorriest bunch you ever saw."

Maisie handed letters over the counter with both hands as she talked.

"Here's something special for you, Sue, and the same old regular for Jo, and I guess I'll give this one to you, Angel, since Cupid kind of passed you by today. It's addressed to all three of you—from Fort Oglethorpe."

"It's from Pete," squealed Sue, ripping off the envelope of the V-letter she held in her hand and waving it excitedly under Jo's nose. "And here's word from Johnny. Gosh, that's quick time—he's only been gone two weeks. I take it he's in England."

Rapidly Sue read the few lines on the single sheet of her

V-mail, while Jo tucked her letter from Bill into the pocket of her shirt until she could read it in quieter surroundings.

"Let's get out of here and give someone else a chance," suggested Angela quietly. "See you later, Maisie. Thanks for the candy and the decorations."

"Don't thank me. They don't come out of my pocket. Everybody antes up for the snack bowl, you know."

"Yes, but everybody doesn't sit up overtime making decorations. 'By now."

"She's quite a girl, that little Maisie," said Jo as they wandered toward the dayroom, where they could listen to Pete's letter without being disturbed. "Heaven knows mail call is the most popular moment of the day, bar none—"

"Excepting chow," protested Sue.

"No, not even excepting chow. I was going to say, when so rudely interrupted, that when you get the letter you want so badly—or any at all—you hardly notice what the mail-room looks like. But I know that cute old Maisie has given a lift to many a gal who didn't get a letter, with her jokes and her bowl of candy and the cheerful way she fixes things up over there. She's quite a psychologist."

"Trust you to figure it out, Josie. I just took it for granted that the mailroom was always a cheerful place because Maisie is such a good old egg."

"And because you haven't been looking in vain for a letter that didn't come, perhaps. Wait until your precious Johnny skips a few days or weeks, or mail is held up, as Bill's letters were once for five weeks, and you'll know what a real job Maisie has on her hands."

Sue laughed as she tucked her V-mail letter into her shoulder bag.

"If this is a sample of Johnny's letter writing—and he warned me he wasn't much of a hand at it—I won't be weeping on Maisie's shoulder, I betcha. 'I'm here—I wish

I was there. Don't take any wooden money—all my love—Johnny.' Period."

"That says just about everything, doesn't it?" asked Angela soberly.

Jo looked quickly at her as they settled themselves in a corner of the almost deserted dayroom. She wondered, as she had many times recently, if Angel was working too hard. She had always been the quietest member of their little group, but there had been something of strain and unhappiness in her face and manner lately that was unlike Angel. In spite of the fact that she was a year or two younger, Jo felt older and somehow responsible for keeping an eye on both Angel and Sue. There were still many times when Sue needed steadying. Now, she decided, Angel needed to be brought out of her absorption with her job.

As different as their work was, there were not so many opportunities to get together as there had been when they were in training together. She wondered, too, if she were imagining that a coolness had grown up between Sue and Angel or if, being roommates, they sometimes rubbed each other the wrong way. However, there was no time now to think about this problem, if it were one, for Angel had opened Pete's thick letter and had told Sue a little sharply that she'd better settle down if they were going to have time to read it together before going back to barracks to polish up their equipment for the big event later in the afternoon.

Sue caught the snapshots that fell from the envelope as Angela smoothed out the crackling pages covered with Pete's loose-jointed characteristic scrawl.

"I'd shoot anyone who tried to take a picture of me in a gas mask or coveralls," she said as she studied the prints. "Remember our first alert and how disgusted Captain Cramer was with our performance? Boy, she doesn't need to be ashamed of us now! I can put that old mask on in nothing flat in spite of bobby pins, hair-do, and pitch blackness. I wonder if gas really will be used in this war?"

"If it is, we'll be ready for it. But let's hear what Pete has to say about that. She ought to know; for she's in it up to her neck apparently, and crazy about it."

The girls settled themselves comfortably as Angela began to read, seeing plainly Pete's round face and animated gestures as they listened to her account of her job as instructor in chemical warfare.

"Dear B's:

"The enclosed exhibits are from my own private chamber of horrors. I hope they give you a good laugh, though I assure you the life of a gas noncommissioned officer is no laughing matter. Yes, that's what I'm called—though the freezing of ranks keeps me still a Private First Class, you old Corporals and Sergeants, you!

"My diploma from the three weeks' specialist course in chemical warfare (enclosed and please return—it's precious) may look like a sheet of funnies, but I assure you it's the real thing and was the cause of removing pounds and pounds from your Pete—all of which I have since regained in spite of my strenuous daily schedule. As my Mom always says 'Land sakes, I'm just as thin as I can be'— meaning she'll never be any less hefty, thank goodness.

"The course was tremendously interesting and I learned so much I'm fairly bursting at the seams. No cracks please. There were one hundred four men in the course and only four WACs (pardon me if I drop out the extra A a few days ahead of time—I have to get in practice). And, by the way, I was darn glad to hear that you all decided to reenlist in the Corps and not take the opportunity of quitting at this momentous moment, as a few lily-livered women did!

Almost by the time you receive this autobiography we'll have our WAC service ribbons and I for one am going to be mighty proud to wear that little green and gold bar. Wish we could all take our oath together, but I'll be thinking about you anyhow. I hope you haven't given up the idea of our getting together one of these days, though how we could all manage a furlough at the same time in this unpredictable Army I don't know. I suppose Ann Dudley has kept in touch with you, as she has with me. Remember our talk fest in the pine woods at the Fort last February? My gosh, that seems years ago and a lifetime away, doesn't it?

"Before I go into a dissertation on my favorite subject—though, from what Sue wrote about hating the occasional gas drills you folks go through, you may not be interested—I wonder if you have had any lessons in Judo—unarmed defense. Right now we are in the thick of it, so I'm giving you fair warning, Sue, not to pick a fight with me when we get together. We have been learning wrist holds, choking, and defense against kicks. We all have an array of scars due to overlong fingernails encountered in practice, but it is fascinating and everyone is very interested in learning the art. Who knows? After the war we girls may not need to take along mad-money on some of our dates. If a guy gets too fresh—give him the old Judo tricks and he'll be the one limping home on foot, if he *can* limp.

"Well, to get on to the job. It's a little hard to write, for I have a very tender wrist due to a little mishap involving a tiny spot of mustard gas. I look as if I had a concentrated dose of poison ivy, but I'm sort of proud of my wounds at that. Imagine how proud I'll be when my grandchildren ask me how I got those scars. The dear old lady dressed in lavender will yank her lace cap down over one eye and say proudly, 'Why, chillun, them's souvenirs of
146

your Gramma's soldier days way back yonder when she was teachin' rookies to cook with gas, by cricky!'

"I won't be technical, though I know a lot of words I had never heard of a few short months ago. Lacrimators (tear makers) are called harassing agents, with wonderful names like chloracetophenone (smells like apple blossoms) and brombenzyl-cyanide (smells like sour fruit). Vesicants (blister gases) and lung irritants are called casualty agents, with names such as phosgene (smells like musty hay, green corn, or ensilage) and mustard, of course (which, strangely enough, smells like mustard—or garlic or horseradish!).

"I could go on for hours about them and tell you about the symbols and colors used to designate each one, but I'm afraid you'd stop reading. I was scared to death of this stuff at first and was sunk when I was told I was to go to the chemical-warfare school. Now I really love it and, of course, I'm hoping that eventually I'll be accepted as a gas noncommissioned officer in a company sent overseas. Meanwhile I plug along and am having the time of my life.

"Here's a little group of verses that we use to learn the various agents, and believe me they come in handy:

> Father was pleased that Sunday morn
> To note the aroma of fresh-cut corn.
> Cried little Willie, turning green,
> "Grab your mask, Pop, that's Phosgene."

> Apple blossoms lend their smell
> To the sadness of farewell.
> It's O.K. if you feel blue,
> But tear gas sets you sobbing too.
>   [Chloracetophenone]

> Said the flypaper to the fly,
> "You look sick enough to die.

That ain't Flit you've chanced to sniff,
It's Chlorpicrin, one small whiff."

Grandma smelled geranium,
Started feeling kinda bum.
Thought she'd had a garden blight,
What she'd found was Lewisite.

[Blister gas]

"How would you like to take a week's trip through
my 'gasworks'? Here's what I did last week—a typical one.

"To begin with, there were four companies to take the
six-hour course. On Monday I had Company 13 for the
first hour of the course. In this course we begin by explain-
ing the gas mask. (Yes, I know you've had some of this; but
we are a lot more thorough than we were when we had
basic.) We give them the entire nomenclature and the func-
tion of each part. Then we trace the workings of the mask.
Then I stand on a chair (because I'm still short—wish I'd
grow *up* instead of sideways) and demonstrate the proper
method of slinging and unslinging the carrier and putting
the mask on the face, adjusting the mask to the individual,
and removing and replacing the mask. Then comes the practice of all this for the rest of the hour and the poor gals
discover they have too many thumbs and too much hair,
that their noses are too big and their precious bobby pins
are a nuisance. I still get a big laugh out of that first hour.
All this is repeated on Monday for the other three companies. I could handle a gas mask by this time at the bottom
of a swimming pool with both hands tied behind me, I betcha.

"On Tuesday the second hour of the course was a lec-
ture—don't laugh—by me on the chemical agents themselves—their chemical properties and the physical, tactical,
and psychological uses of each. We tell them the first aid
for each agent, the odor of and protection against each one.

148

Diploma from an Army specialists' course in chemical warfare, picturing the final lengthy practice tests in which WAC students participated, strenuous obstacles excepted.

"Wednesday is 'detonation day.' The companies are taken into the field, where we set up a field detonation. We set off the four principal casualty agents (in a concentration of alcohol for training purposes). They are strong enough to give off the odors but not enough to cause casualties, naturally. To set them off, detonators are attached to glass tubes and wired to a blasting machine. A rheostat is used to check the circuit.

"Then we set off a thermite and a magnesium bomb (incendiaries) and the troops are shown the proper method of handling same.

"The fourth and fifth hours of the course are taken up with the gas-chamber exercise. The troops go through a concentration of tear gas (harmless) and prove the effectiveness of the gas mask. At this point the careless ones resolve to practice getting their masks on, and how!

"My clothes are so saturated at the end of this part of the course that when I take my mask off I cry all the way home from the fumes still coming off the clothes. The girls in the barracks call me either 'sad sack' or 'stinky' most of the time.

"On Friday we finish the course with an hour of 'decontamination.' This includes individual and collective protection methods of decontaminating food, property, and individuals and detecting the effectiveness of decontamination. Decontamination, dear students, is the process whereby a chemical agent is partially or completely neutralized, destroyed, or removed.

"By this time you'll be ready to slay me, but I've really gone into this much detail hoping you'll send this on to Ann Dudley for me. I don't have much time to write letters, as you can see from the above schedule, so I have to use the old round-robin method for correspondence.

"But don't think my life is all lived behind a gas mask,

please. Right now we are getting up a *Bomb Shell Revue* that may not be Broadway timbre, but I bet we won't need to explode tear-gas bombs to make 'em laugh till they cry.

"Also, ahem, there is a certain six-foot corporal who's formed a pleasant habit of leavening this mass of doughgirls. Excuse it please, Josie. Nothing serious, so far. But a girl can dream, can't she? Remember—our proportion of women to men on this post is in reverse ratio to yours, and a date is usually a big occasion. Ho hum! Sometimes I wonder what we used to find to talk about to our boy friends before the war. Harry and I argue sometimes about how many floating smoke pots would be needed to provide a thirty-minute smoke screen to cover a ranger battalion in a hit-and-run landing attack on a thousand-yard beach frontage— with even more zest than I remember in football arguments with Tom and Dick in the old days.

"And I suppose you WACs in the AAF and your dates watch the red and green lights of planes in the sky over your field on clear nights instead of star gazing. Oh, I don't mean there aren't the usual things to talk about, too, but it does make a difference when you're living the same kind of life as the men on a more or less isolated Army post.

"I wish you three would loosen up and bring me up to date about yourselves, your jobs, and your heart interests. I noted in Sue's letter, a month ago, some enthusiasm, I thought, about one Johnny Samson and a tantalizing reference to an awakening interest on Angel's part in somebody or other. Jo, I take it, is still faithful to Bill Garland.

"It's almost time for chow and I'm still in my monkey suit, so I'll have to stop. Am doing the movies tonight with Harry—*Lady in the Dark,* because he's crazy about Ginger Rogers. Stiff competition for me, maybe; but he's pretty swell to me, so I should worry about glamour.

"Write soon now to your Pete."

151

"She certainly shows us up when it comes to writing a letter, doesn't she? It's your turn to answer her, Angel, and I hope you give her chemical for chemical! Let's pick out all the technical terms we can think of and make her head spin as mine is after all those chloro-phenone-brombenzoodiacs. Gosh, it's getting late, gals. I've got to scoot over to the PX to buy a new tie before I can join the Army. See you later."

"Why don't we have supper at the Noncom Club tonight and go to the movies together to celebrate?" suggested Jo as Sue started for the door.

"Swell idea—for supper anyhow. But I promised Charlie Langtree I'd go to the first show with him. Sorry."

With a nonchalant wave of her hand Sue disappeared on the double quick, for it was quite a walk to the Post Exchange from their area.

Angela -slumped against the back of the divan and closed her eyes as if she were too weary to face the period of drill and the induction ceremony that was to follow it.

"Why don't you go over to the barracks and take a short nap, Angel? You'll have time. Lucky we didn't have to work this afternoon and go through all this other business too. I'll press anything you have to have when I do mine. You look worn out."

"Oh, I'm not tired."

Angela's attempt at a smiling denial was so unsuccessful that Jo laid a hand on her knee and gave her a gentle shake.

"Don't you think you'd better tell me what's bothering you? Something is—I'm sure of it. I have my own idea, of course, but I may be wrong."

Angela was silent, but she did not draw away from the comforting pressure of the hand on her knee; so after a moment Jo continued.

152

"I walked home with Charlie Langtree a couple of nights ago. He didn't come right out and ask me, but I imagined he wasn't feeling too good about your breaking a couple of dates with him on account of having to work late at the laboratory. In fact, he seemed to feel you had made work an excuse. I knew that wasn't true and I told him so."

"You can't blame him for preferring Sue's company to mine," said Angela in a smothered voice. "I did have to work, both those times! It didn't take Sue long to forget Johnny, did it?"

"Now listen, Angel. Sue hasn't forgotten Johnny. Why, they're practically engaged—would be, I guess, if he hadn't been shipped out so suddenly. Charlie is just somebody to have fun with as far as she's concerned. You don't see me sitting home over a book every night just because my Bill isn't here, do you? Besides, I happen to know Sue thinks that Lieutenant Cooper's interest in you isn't entirely professional; and she's been worrying about it because of the blamed old taboo about dating officers. Don't be a mouse. If you like Sergeant Langtree—and I used to think you did and I'm darned sure he likes you—buck up and give the lad a chance."

"It's too late now. I don't quite see myself competing with Susie."

Angela's bitter tone was so unlike her that Jo looked at her with a worried frown. With anyone less sensitive it would have been a fairly simple matter to clear up what had plainly been a misunderstanding. Angela hadn't even noticed the reference to Lieutenant Cooper apparently, but it was clear that she did feel deeply about the attractive radio operator's attentions to her sociable roommate.

After a moment's silence Angela opened her eyes and smiled at Jo in quite her old fashion.

"I didn't realize I was wearing my heart on my sleeve," she admitted. "Perhaps I was taking Charlie's interest too much for granted. He was pretty attentive, you know. But he certainly isn't shy or sensitive—why, I've never known a more considerate, even-tempered fellow or one that was as much fun and, well, sort of masterful." Angela hesitated over the last word and a flush crept into her cheeks as she looked appealingly at Jo. "In other words, he's the kind that wouldn't be discouraged by someone's breaking a few dates—especially when it wasn't done deliberately."

"He's also mighty independent, Angel, and shy, really. Why, when Sue and I first worked with him in the radio section, he acted scared to death of us. We used to call him old Lankylegs. If he thought you preferred a pair of silver bars to a sergeant's rating, he'd say to hell with you—if I know Charlie."

"But I can't say that to the head of my department, Jo. You know yourself how hard it is to manage some of your pilots who don't give a continental about taboos. It's different for you, in some ways. You can go flying with them because it's part of your job to take operational flights; but I don't see you making dates with them, no matter how many opportunities you have to do so."

Jo smiled reminiscently.

"You're quite right. I've learned to be very devious and quick-witted in order to say no without coming right out with the real reason. It's kind of hard, too, for they're so darned cute sometimes. Well, we've got to get going, Angel-Face. But don't forget what Aunt Josie's been telling you. It's stupid for you and Sue to build up a misunderstanding about nothing. She'd have a fit if she knew the straight of the situation."

"I'll never forgive you if you tell her."

On August 6, 1943, the Women's Army Auxiliary Corps became the Women's Army Corps. In this photograph, the enlisted women of the first WAC detachment at Mitchell Field, New York, are shown being inducted into the Army of the United States as members of the Women's Army Corps.

Angela's blue eyes deepened as they demanded a promise of silence from Jo, but the look of strain had left them.

"O.K., but you've got to do your part and act like a human being instead of an icicle the next time you see Charlie. If you do, it won't be necessary to tell anybody anything."

"I hope you're right. It's funny, but I feel better about it already and a little while ago I thought I would die before I'd admit I was working myself up to a first-class heartache. You're such a comfort."

"Honesty is the best policy—with someone you can trust, and you know you can trust me. Do you think you can say 'I do' to the Army now with real enthusiasm this afternoon?"

"I certainly can. And yet nothing has actually changed except my own point of view. You are a magician, Josie."

"Don't give me any credit; I was just the—what did Pete call it?—the plunger on the battery that set off the detonation. Or maybe the decontamination squad."

"You are a nice fresh breeze that blew away an enemy smoke screen, I think! I can't wait to fill Pete's ears with photographic formulas. I'll fix her!"

"And I'll give her a dose of adiabatic lapse rates, stable and instable conditions, isobars, isotherms, and isosteres that will make her holler 'uncle,' " Jo promised as they set off for the barracks in high spirits to prepare for the induction ceremony that would make them a fully accepted unit of the great Army of the United States of America.

A cooling breeze from the ocean lifted the drooping folds of the garrison flag and freshened the oppressive atmosphere as the slender column of khaki-clad figures swung down the parade ground in the late afternoon of that historic August 6, 1943. The tedium of the past three hours of preparation

156

and standing about waiting for the final orders that would bring them before the commandant of the post were forgotten now in the sudden tenseness of this long-awaited moment.

Faultlessly the platoon leaders swung their units into line facing the colonel, his staff, and the officers of the company. Unsmiling and stern, the colonel addressed the hundred straight figures standing at attention before him. With simple ringing words he thanked them for their devotion to duty as members of the Women's Auxiliary Army Corps and for the immeasurable service rendered his post in the past few months.

"My highest praise and compliments and thanks belong to you women and to your officers for the part you have already played in all aspects of our life on this field. I look forward to the day when your ranks are increased tenfold. We need you and women like you and I am proud to administer the oath of allegiance to you that will make you an honored part of the Army of the United States of America, to which I have given the best years of my life and found them good years. You will now repeat after me this oath:

"I, ———, a citizen of the United States, do hereby acknowledge to have voluntarily enlisted this sixth day of August, 1943, in the Women's Army Corps, Army of the United States of America, for the period of the duration of the war and six months thereafter under the conditions prescribed by law, unless sooner discharged by proper authority; and do also agree to accept from the United States such bounty, pay, rations, and clothing as are or may be established by law. And I do solemnly swear (or affirm) that I will bear true faith and allegiance to the United States of America; that I will serve them honestly and faithfully against all their enemies whomsoever; and that I will obey

157

the orders of the President of the United States, and the orders of the officers appointed over me, according to the Rules and Articles of War."

The whole ceremony took only a few minutes, but its very brevity and simplicity added to its impressiveness as with raised right hands the light voices of the women gave back the solemn words in a swelling chorus to the colonel:

". . . I will bear true faith and allegiance to the United States of America . . . I will serve them honestly and faithfully against all their enemies whomsoever . . ."

CHAPTER XII

"Full Speed Ahead"

Inside the glass-enclosed control tower at the edge of the wide field Sue looked up from the maze of dials in front of her and glanced at her wrist watch. Twenty minutes to twelve—maybe that accounted for the momentary lull in the constant aerial conversation that had characterized this fine clear May morning. After a week of stubborn fog, which had grounded all planes at the field, the cheerful activity was a relief to Sue as she sat in the midst of a jabber of unseen voices that gave their demands and reports through a din of crackling static.

Automatically she reached with one hand for the field glasses at her elbow, for out of the welter of voices she had detected the one directed at her. With the other hand she picked up the French telephone receiver that was her microphone. After searching the sky for a moment with the glasses she seemed satisfied, for she laid them aside and spoke into the microphone—answering the pilot of the plane, who had called the tower for instructions about landing.

"We have you in sight. You are cleared to land on runway three. Call the tower when turning into final. Over."

"O.K., Sarge. Say, I've got a friend of yours on board— furlough hitchhiker from Fort Oglethorpe. I'll bring her up to the tower when we've checked in."

The pilot's breezy nonchalance brought a grin to Sue's

159

face, but her tone was businesslike as she guided the transport plane in for a landing under the supervision of the noncom in charge of the tower.

During the next few minutes she was too busy to think about anything but the job at hand. Her duty for the day was over at twelve, and she would then be free until six o'clock the next morning.

Close upon the heels of her relief came the pilot of the transport plane she had guided to a landing—with Dorothy Peterson in tow, who was still all but speechless from the excitement of her first airplane trip and the fulfillment of a long-hoped-for plan to visit the Three B's at their base.

Subdued and somewhat awed at being so close to the heart of the great airfield, Pete's meeting with Sue was much more casual than the one she had pictured after a year of separation. She listened with polite interest while Sue explained the functions of the control tower and its equipment with formal preciseness.

"I don't see how you make head or tail of anything in this racket," Pete confessed finally. "What with weather reports coming in over the teletalk and planes zooming up and booming down, I should think you'd go nuts."

"It's all very orderly, really, and you get used to the noise eventually. Weather reports come in regularly every hour on the half hour over the teletalk, which is kept clear at that time for that purpose, and are taken down on these charts. That's part of my job usually. I don't often get a chance to be in A Position as I was this morning when your plane came in. When we aren't too busy the sergeant in charge lets me take over, but you bet he is right at my elbow all the time. Usually I am in B Position, which is plenty busy and important too. Only the man in A Position talks to the planes, giving them directions for landing or taxiing

The work of the control tower, from which all the air traffic of an airplane base is directed, is so exacting that only persons with special aptitudes and training are accepted for duty.

into position for the take-off. We also handle all the records that are played over the public-address system—bugle calls, music, and so forth. There is plenty to do for the three of us who are on duty here in the tower."

"What if you have six or seven planes all calling the tower at once for a landing? Who comes down first?"

"There are very strict priorities in that case. A plane in distress of any kind gets first attention, naturally, no matter what type or size it is. Otherwise the big fellows are brought down first and the others are given an altitude to maintain until they are ordered down to a certain runway at a certain moment. It's just a matter of good old traffic regulation, really, whether they are going up or coming down. It's fun to direct a pilot when he is taxiing into position for the take-off, especially if he isn't too familiar with the field and its runways. You just keep on talking to him 'straight ahead to so-and-so, turn left, turn right,' until he is on the proper runway. Or else he simply tags along behind one of those little jeeps I pointed out to you a moment ago. I always get a laugh out of one of those little bugs scooting along with a big old plane trundling behind the sassy 'Follow Me' painted on the back of the car."

"But what if a plane's radio is out of whack and the pilot can't talk to the tower?"

"We tell him to waggle a wing or something like that to show he is getting our signals. Not long ago a pilot told us to waggle the tower if we got his signals all right! If anything happens to our communications system we use the blinker light to direct him, and sometimes we use it anyway. The men have to know all possible tricks, of course, that will help them under battle conditions. They won't always be taking off and landing from a peaceful field like this one. Even here we have emergencies and we have to be prepared for them. It is a mighty responsible job, being in the control

162

tower, and the first thing you have to do is learn to control yourself."

On the way down from the tower Sue dropped her almost stilted manner and hugged Pete in a wholly natural and enthusiastic way before guiding her out of the building.

"Gosh, I began to think you'd gotten the swell head or something," gasped Pete, straightening her hat and pulling down her blouse after Sue's onslaught.

"I was on my good behavior with Lieutenant Norris present," chuckled Sue. "He's swell; but he has ears in the back of his head, no matter how much din there is. I knew he'd pick me up tomorrow if my explanations to you weren't up to scratch."

"You must be pretty good to do a job like yours. And, my, my, you look as spick-and-span as a fashion plate! You ought to see me at the end of a day's work—I usually look like a chimney sweep in my stained old monkey suit."

"You should have seen me in my tearing-radios-apart days. I've had my share of dirty work, don't worry, and so has Jo—she still has."

"Your radio training probably was a help in getting you your job in the control tower, wasn't it?"

"It's been a help since I've been on the job, yes. But I did a lot of other things first. I was scared I wouldn't make good for a while. I'm not exactly phlegmatic and calm, you know. With an officer like Lieutenant Norris you just naturally do your darnedest to live up to his expectations. Now Jo would be A-1, no matter how easygoing her boss might be; but I guess I need the tough kind to keep me on my toes. I used to think some of the boys whom I've talked to when they come back from overseas were sort of hero worshipers about some of their officers, but I don't now. I'd go through most anything for that little old sandy-haired lieutenant."

"My chemical officer is like that," agreed Pete enthusiastically. "I guess I wouldn't be so fond of my old gasworks if she weren't so darned smart and fair and human all at the same time. But then most of our officers down at the Fort are pretty swell. Is that where Ann and I will be watching the big doings from this afternoon? She is coming, isn't she?"

Pete indicated the bleachers on the far side of the parade ground as they hurried on the double-quick toward the WAC area.

"You still fire both barrels at once, I see. The answer is 'Yes,' squared. Unless you'd like to march in the second platoon along with Angel, Jo, and me. Ann is probably in the mess hall already with Captain Cramer, who invited her to have lunch there with her and some other officers. We're invited to join them if you'd like."

"Too much brass for me, if you don't mind. Anyhow we're a little late, aren't we?"

"Maybe so; but Captain Cramer is really swell, so don't let that bother you. She's been through a lot with us since our first hundred WACs landed here about a year ago. This second anniversary of the Corps is a double celebration for some of the members of the detachment. Why don't you march with us, Petie? Jo is our platoon sergeant, you know, and the best there is, of course. It would seem like old times to have you puffing along beside me when we have to stretch our short legs on the wide turns."

"No, thanks. I'm on furlough, remember. Come to think of it, I guess it's the first time I've had a chance to be on the side lines and watch WACs go through their paces. You'd better be good, too, for I won't miss a trick."

"Gosh, you make me nervous! Just remember, though, we're too darn busy on the job to do as much drilling as you folks do down yonder. But you watch the second platoon and I'll guarantee you won't feel disgraced. We ought to

164

be first, by rights. We're lots better. And, as for feeling superior about wearing our propeller and wings. you don't seem exactly ashamed of the crossed retorts on your collar, you old incendiary bomb."

"What time is the parade?" asked Pete as they entered Sue's barracks.

"Two o'clock, and this place will be a madhouse for the next hour; for everybody has to report to our drill area at one in class A uniforms. It's been a madhouse for the last two days, for that matter, getting ready for general inspection. These old barracks were scrubbed from roof to floor boards, and I mean literally—walls, windows, and ceilings. Come along now or we'll miss chow. I bet Angel and Jo are wondering if your promise to be here was all a bluff. I can't wait to tell them that I personally guided your plane to a landing. We had an idea you might be able to catch a ride up, but of course you never can tell. I haven't seen Ann yet and I'm dying to."

Sue rattled on at such a rate all the time she was storing the visitor's belongings away that Pete hadn't a chance to get a word in edgewise. She still felt somewhat dizzy from the plane trip, during which she had experienced a slight attack of air sickness. Perhaps that was why she felt reluctant to face a mess hall full of strange faces when greeting her friends for the first time after months of separation.

"I bet you are starved," Sue said as she hurried Pete with her washing up. "I'll be glad when this old parade is over, darn it. Angel and Jo and I made a solemn agreement that whoever got ahold of you or Ann first would wait until we were all together to get the news and give it. And me just busting to tell you about— Hush your mouth, chile," she scolded herself.

"I've got some news I'm bursting seams with, too," began Pete, but Sue laid a finger on her lips warningly.

"Don't tell me! I think it's a silly agreement myself—still it will be more fun to wait till the shenanigans are over. We can let down our hair at Ann's tonight. A friend of hers in a town five miles from here has turned over her house to her for tonight and cleared out lock, stock, and barrel. Isn't that just like Ann, to dig up a real reunion spot? We're all going over there when we get through this afternoon. By some minor or major miracle all three of us managed to get late passes at the same time."

Sue's explanation given earlier would have spared her some uncomfortable moments, thought Pete, her spirits rising perceptibly.

"It always takes me a little while to get used to being on leave," she said almost shyly as they hurried over to the mess hall. "I feel guilty at being so lazy, until I get used to the idea. I wonder what it will be like when the war's over. Maybe we won't relish being civilians again."

"You'd better change your mind and march with the platoon this afternoon if being on furlough makes you uncomfortable. You're going to be mighty envious when you see how hot and tired everybody is after an hour of practice drill and another hour of hutting around that parade ground in this sticky heat. The Corps is two years old. So what?"

For a moment such indifference from Sue about an anniversary that she had regarded as a momentous occasion for her beloved Corps dismayed Pete until she remembered Sue's habit of grumbling.

"You *must* be hungry," she said, smiling at Sue until her frown lifted.

"I never put anything over on you three, do I? I'm bursting with pride and joy, the same as you are! Let's eat."

At two o'clock sharp Pete laid a hand on Ann's arm and said quietly, "There they come."

At busy Stewart Field—where cadets from the United States Military Academy learn to fly, one of the busiest places is Base Operations. Here hundreds of flights daily are planned and scheduled and dispatched. Alert, efficient WAC's help "keep 'em flying."

Following the direction of Pete's gesture, Ann turned her eyes away from the planes that circled the field on the far side of the hangar line—to watch the long column of khaki-clad figures, eight abreast, as it swung into the macadam road bordering the parade ground.

"Where's the band?" Ann whispered, amazed that the other onlookers who filled the temporary bleachers were still talking briskly and loudly.

Pete nodded her head in the direction of the hangar line, where she had seen a flash of instruments in the sun.

"It will meet them at the end of this road. We have our own WAC band at the Fort, remember?"

"Indeed I do. I'll never forget your wonderful review on that very special occasion. It seems years ago, doesn't it?"

"Not to me, it doesn't. These months in the Corps have gone by like—like that plane up there that just took off. Look—it's almost out of sight."

"You've never been sorry you reenlisted last August, then?"

"Gracious, no! Why, it never even entered my head to leave when we were given the chance to do so. Even if I had been tempted to, as I know Jo and Sue were, I would have stayed on for the same reason they did."

"I didn't know they had considered seriously not reenlisting," said Ann, her eyes on the advancing column that was still some distance from them.

"Plenty of us thought about it, Ann. It's not exactly an easy life, you know, even when you love it as much as I do. I guess girls like Sue and Jo just couldn't see themselves quitting something they had started, as long as they were still needed."

Pete stood up for a better view of the marchers, watching the even ranks closely.

"Not bad," she murmured as Ann balanced precariously

168

beside her. "For Air WACs," she added, with a mischievous grin.

At the intersection of the roads that bordered the parade ground, the post band, preceded by the WAC Color Guard, struck up a military march and led the four platoons of a hundred each onto the field. At a short distance in front of the flagpole it halted and continued to play while the column swept down the field almost to the farthest end.

With smooth perfection the long column was maneuvered into position by their platoon officers, until a line of forty-eight WACs, arms' length apart and eight ranks deep, stood at attention facing the company commander alone in the center of the field.

The band had stopped playing when the first platoon reached the end of the field, and over the green field the officers' orders to the ranks came faintly but clearly on the still air.

In a low voice Pete explained to Ann what the orders were and why the platoon officers and platoon guides kept changing their positions until the ranks were "dressed" in straight, even lines to their complete satisfaction.

"Jo is platoon sergeant of the second platoon, you know. She's standing just behind the platoon guide in the farthest rank. The guides are the only ones still facing away from us. Here comes the adjutant now to make the report to the CO. She has a lot of little dogtrots to make all by herself, you notice. Those are the platoon officers out in front of the platoons, where the white markers are. Guess we'll have 'The Star-Spangled Banner' next and then probably some speeches. I see we have quite a lot of brass down in front. That's the commanding general of this Air Force, I think, and the colonel beside him is commandant of the post."

Pete hardly had finished her sentence when the first notes of the National Anthem brought her and all the military

169

personnel present so rigidly to attention that Ann felt self-consciously lax and informal, though her habitually erect bearing was even straighter than usual.

The speeches that followed the playing of the anthem were brief but laudatory and Pete beamed as she listened.

"I'll bet those gals across the field are getting about one word in fifty," she whispered to Ann. "The public-address system, as usual, leaves room for plenty of improvement."

"Now what?" asked Ann when the speeches were finished and the ranks still stood at parade rest facing the blazing sun.

"A command will probably be given to the band to 'sound off'—march up and down a little and play a good lively tune—and then they'll march back to the area and we'll at last have a chance to do a little chopping together."

"Chopping?"

"Beat the gums—chew the fat—gossip, if you like."

"My vocabulary is out of date," Ann admitted. "I'm afraid we shall have to revise our dictionaries when this war is over. On the whole, though, I can't see that you girls go out of your way to use Army slang. I expected more of it, to tell the truth."

"Maybe we're on our good behavior in front of you, ma'am. We sometimes get careless with our language, living in close quarters the way so many of us do. It must be one of the by-products of war. Gosh, just look at those gals out there—I have to hand it to them—they're good."

With eyes narrowed, Pete watched closely as the four platoons were brought about-face and swung back down the field, passing in review in front of their commanding officer and the reviewing stand.

At the end of the field the columns executed a smart column-left and began the long march back to the WAC area, followed by the spontaneous cheers of the spectators.

There is more to checking a pilot's flight plan than meets the eye in this particular scene, but the WAC whose job it is knows all the details and carries through on them.

The first platoon, upon reaching the bend in the road at the end of the field, made the turn in perfect formation.

In the front ranks of the second platoon, Jo, as platoon sergeant, was suddenly aware that Lieutenant Nolan, the platoon officer, was missing and remembered hearing her say that she would have to slip out of formation and hustle on ahead to show some visiting officers through the area. The second in command, marching eyes-front at Jo's right, was unaware that Lieutenant Nolan was no longer in her place at the far left of the platoon. The turn of the road was very near . . . the turn of the road was under the marching feet, and still no command was given. The white curbing rose at the feet of the front rank . . . the grass beyond was under its feet when Jo took a deep breath and expelled it in a firm command over her shoulder at the surprised ranks behind her, "Column left, Harch."

The leading elements of the platoon moved as one on the turn, not a second too soon and without breaking cadence, in a fancy wide curve that brought a groan of dismay through Jo's clenched teeth.

"I'll never hear the last of this from Pete," she thought grimly, wondering what the second in command would have to say about her wholly unauthorized action.

When the ranks were dismissed at the entrance to the WAC area, however, the officer grinned at her ruefully and praised her for saving the day.

"Thank you, ma'am. I knew I had no business to give the command; but I suddenly realized that you didn't know that Lieutenant Nolan left us just before the turn, and I could just see us landing in Officers' Row if somebody didn't holler out fast."

"I'm sorry it happened when you had visitors looking on. It's the best-drilled platoon in the detachment, Sergeant, thanks to you. Better luck next time."

The huge cafeteria and soda bar where the Three B's had planned to meet Pete and Ann after the parade was so crowded with WACs, soldiers, officers, and civilians that the five friends finally gave up trying to get waited on.

"Why don't we grab a bus and go on over to Ann's place?" demanded Sue as they stood outside of the PX trying to decide what points of interest on the post they would show the visitors first.

Ann had looked forward to seeing something of the work that the girls were doing, but she was quick to realize that they were spoiling to get off the base and have an opportunity to talk in peace and quiet.

"Captain Cramer said she would arrange for a car to take us to town if I would let her know when we were ready," she suggested. "Maybe we can find something special in the way of a celebration in the village. It seems a little dull just to take you to a house for a home-cooked meal on such an occasion as this."

"Listen to her! You don't know what a treat it will be to walk on rugs and see pictures on the walls and curtains at the windows and open a man-sized icebox and drink out of cups with handles. Dull!"

Sue's voice rose in a squeal and the others voiced their enthusiasm with such fervor that Ann was convinced that her arrangements for this long-hoped-for reunion had been well inspired.

"Let's not bother the CO about a car. We can catch a bus and be in the village in ten minutes. I'll run over and grab Pete's and my kit bags and meet you at the gate. It was pretty smart of me to arrange for my day off tomorrow, wasn't it?"

Jo laughed at the face Sue made, remembering that she went on duty the next morning at six o'clock.

"I'll bring Ann and Pete back tomorrow after a nice lazy breakfast and show them the whole blamed works— except, of course, the hangar line and the control tower. Civilians can't go there, so Susie will have to tell you what she does up in her bird cage."

The white clapboarded cottage to which Ann led the way down a wide elm-shaded street was like a dream come true to the girls who had lived for so many long months in stark, antiseptically clean barracks. From the bud-crowded rambler roses that drooped over its tiny entrance porch, the smooth handkerchief lawn, and the flowering shrubs below its casement windows to the spacious back garden enclosed with a spruce-picket fence, it spoke of its owner's care and good taste.

The interior was bright with sunlight and spring flowers so lovingly and skillfully arranged that Angela had eyes for nothing else.

Pete turned from an examination of close-packed book-shelves and record cabinets to Ann with a sigh of utter relaxation.

"Let's stay a week, and just talk and read and listen to good music. You're magical, and generous with friend-ship. I can't tell you what it has meant to me and some of my pals at the Fort to have those friends of yours in Chattanooga share their homes with us—all on account of you. And now you're doing the same thing in sharing this friend and her home.

> "Show me his friends and I the man shall know;
> This wiser turn a larger wisdom lends:
> Show me the books he loves and I shall know
> The man far better than through mortal friends.*

---

* Silas Weir Mitchell, *Books and the Man.*

I don't quite believe that part about his books. I'd hate to have anybody judge me by mine, these days anyhow."

"Meg will be glad to hear that she has enhanced my reputation by lending us her house. She's one of our authors and it was because I had to talk business with her that I had this opportunity to get away from the city and kill two birds with one stone, as I did on my trip to Chattanooga. I'm getting to be a pretty shot, don't you think? Meg's husband is overseas as a war correspondent and I know she will want to have my Three B's over often, now that the ice has been broken. Speaking of ice, I must fix up that liquid refreshment I promised you."

Ann departed for the kitchen so briskly that she missed the significant glances that passed between the Three B's, but Pete caught it and remembered Sue's earlier hint that Angela had special news of some kind. As far as that was concerned, she had a bombshell of her own that she was longing to explode; but so far there had been no opportunity to set it off effectively.

Hours later the red glow of hardwood coals flickered on the faces of Ann, Jo, and Pete as they sat alone in deep chairs in front of the fireplace. The May evening had turned cool enough to warrant Pete's plea for fire and in its soft circle of light the talk had run in a steady, quiet stream.

It had been very late when Angela and Sue finally started on their reluctant way back to the post in order to be on hand for reveille and their early-morning duties.

As Ann leaned forward to stir the coals, Pete stayed her hand.

"Don't break up my ship, please. See it there, just to the left of the center—a big old transport with three funnels. I've been watching it for ten minutes—it sails on so calmly. I can see the smoke coming from its funnels and crowds of people jammed up against the rails. I can almost make out Angel and me way up in front, hung like clothes horses with all our overseas equipment. Ah! It broke in two! I hope that wasn't a torpedo that busted into us."

Pete gave a little shiver and slid from the chair onto the rug at Ann's feet.

From across the village square a deep-toned bell rang out four chimed quarters, followed by the husky, even stroke of the iron tongue.

"Bong! Bong!"

"Two o'clock, children. I ought to get you to bed."

But Pete pinned Ann in her chair by leaning against her knees.

"Not yet, Ann. I'm sorry Angel had to go back to camp. This kind of thing may not happen again for years—for Angel and me, I mean. Put another log on the fire, Josie."

Pete yawned with contentment when Jo had mended the fire and resumed her lazy position in the depths of her chair.

"This is the first time I've had to think, really, since I got my big news about being accepted for overseas duty. I wonder if Angel feels a little scared about it, as I do now that I've had this reminder of what home is really like."

"I don't see how you two kept so quiet about it for so long. I had a feeling something special was in the wind, but when Sue finally blurted it out, before Angel had a chance to announce it herself, I was flabbergasted."

"Me too," confessed Pete. "I was bursting with my own news as soon as I got off that plane this morning, but Sue told me sternly that all items of importance had to be kept until the witching hour or whatever. I almost forgot about it meanwhile. Of course, I still don't believe it. Maybe that's one reason it wasn't hard to keep quiet about it. I thought I would electrify you all with my announcement and hog the whole spotlight, and then bingo! All I could do was mutter 'Me too'! Wouldn't it be funny if we really did set off on a ship together, like that picture in the coals I saw?"

"Maybe you'll be flown over. Some WACs have gone over that way," suggested Jo slyly, knowing that Pete didn't share the enthusiasm of the Three B's for flying.

"I hope not. It's a good thing I'm not in the Air Forces. I'm strictly earthbound and glad of it."

"You'd get over that if you were in the AAF, I betcha. Of course we don't actually fly planes, but an awful lot of us work on and in and around them all the time. We practically sleep and eat planes. It's catching."

"So I've noticed. I've hardly been able to get a word in edgewise all evening, what with you three gabbling about your favorite ships and pilots—a regular fusillade of fuselages, wasn't it, Ann?"

"It was a wonderful inventory," agreed Ann, with a chuckle. "I only hope I can remember everything I've learned tonight. I'm mighty proud of my four chicks and I want the very best for all of you. I hope the time will soon come when homes like this one will be waiting for Angela and her sergeant and Sue and Johnny Samson. How about you, Pete? I didn't hear you say very much about your affairs of the heart."

"There's nothing much to say, so far. Before I get serious about anybody, I want to see him in civvies and in a peacetime background. There's a long hard row to hoe before I start making ruffled curtains like these cute dimity things of Meg's. It's different with Jo. There's always been Bill apparently, and I'm darned glad he'll soon be on this side again, Josie. That was about the best news I heard tonight, old-timer."

Pete reached out a lazy hand to pat Jo's knee, and settled herself more comfortably against Ann's knees.

"As far as Sue is concerned, I bet she changes her mind a dozen times before she settles down. Maybe Johnny Samson's the one, but she's pretty bighearted. Look how she nearly gummed up things between Angel and her sergeant. If it had been me, I think I would have hauled off and busted her one in the nose."

"More likely in the sergeant's nose, if I know you, Petie. Angel was just making up a good story for your benefit, so don't blame Sue. Besides, she had us worried because we thought she was pretty fond of Lieutenant Cooper. Not just because he's an officer—after all, a mere matter of rank can't keep two people from falling in love, you know. Angel admired the lieutenant because he knew his business and saw to it that his WACs learned all he could teach them in the photo lab. In fact, I think he helped Angel get this overseas assignment, though he told her in the beginning there wasn't a ghost of a chance for her. Look how crazy Sue is about her Lieutenant Norris—in a perfectly impersonal way, of course—and for the same reasons. I feel the same way about Corporal Jensen, who has taught me everything I know about the Link trainer. I wouldn't be an instructor first class today if it hadn't been for him. Love is quite a different matter."

"Looks like the real thing for Angel at any rate."

Pete sat up to poke the fire and tapped the poker on the hearth almost absent-mindedly.

Jo chuckled suddenly, recognizing the letters that the poker in Pete's hands spelled out.

"Did Angel show you the handkerchief she received from Charlie this morning?" she asked him.

"Yes. Didn't you hear her scream with indignation when I asked her if he had embroidered their initials on it?"

"Didn't she show you the dit-dah message in the center of it? Pete's tapping it out on the hearth—dot-dot, dot-dash-dot-dot, dash-dash-dash, dot-dot-dot-dash, dot, dash-dot-dash-dash, dash-dash-dash, dot-dot-dash! Just a radio operator's way of saying 'I love you.'"

"Gee, you've really learned something since you've been in the AAF, haven't you?"

Pete laughed as she replaced the poker and rose nimbly to her feet.

"Now that we have everybody's love affairs straightened out, I think we'd better let Ann get to bed. I bet you could kill us for keeping you up so late, couldn't you?"

"Certainly not, though it is a little 'early' for an old lady like me to be astir. I don't believe I could take the strenuous life that doesn't seem to faze you youngsters. Would you still recommend the Corps to me—if I were a few years younger, that is?"

"Well, ma'am, I think I would. We need a lot more women than we have. It's not an easy life, and rare evenings like this one make you realize pretty keenly how you miss home and all the things it stands for. I love being a WAC, as you know, but I won't be sorry to be a civilian again. I guess mighty few people—men or women—would really like being in the armed forces as a steady diet. But we've got a job to do and, heck, you don't waste much time moaning about it. You just do your job the best way you can, and know the war will be over one of these days."

"The first time I met you, you quoted a verse to us— 'Spring Came on Forever.' Remember? What you have just said reminds me of Browning's lines in 'Asolando'; for it describes you, I think.

"One who never turned his back but marched breast forward,
  Never doubted clouds would break,
  Never dreamed, though right were worsted, wrong would triumph,
  Held we fall to rise, are baffled to fight better,
  Sleep to wake."

"I'm glad you like that verse, Ann, and that you thought of it just now. It has kept me marching forward at times when I felt like skedaddling to the rear—I'll tell you that. But there'll be no waking if we don't get to sleeping, Josie. For'ard. Harch!"

With a brisk poke at Jo to hide a sudden rush of feeling, Pete marched toward the stairs that led to the bedroom under the eaves.

"I hope somebody remembers to give the command for column-left," she shouted over her shoulder. "I'd hate to keep on going through Meg's wall."

When she was abreast of the stair well Jo barked "Squad left, march," so sharply that Ann jumped.

"What is all this about?" she asked, seeing Pete's impish grin and Jo's hand raised to swat her round rear as she began to mount the stairs.

"Squad, halt!"

Pete stopped so abruptly that she almost sat back on Jo's knee that was raised to meet the step close behind her.

The two girls hung over the banister, blowing kisses down at Ann's questioning face.

"Remember the fancy maneuver our platoon executed this afternoon when we almost climbed into the hangar line? I nearly died of mortification, with the base commander and Pete looking on."

"I didn't notice anything wrong. I thought you were perfect."

"And Pete didn't crow about it?"

Jo sounded incredulous as she looked from Pete to Ann and back again.

"I couldn't bear to disillusion her," giggled Pete, scrambling up the stairs on all fours.

"I'll disillusion you, with a hairbrush," threatened Jo, following hot on her trail.

For a long moment Ann stood looking after them. She turned away and stood staring down into the fireplace, trying to find Pete's ship in the dying coals.

"God bless them all, every one—wherever they are, whatever they do—all of our boys and girls . . . and bring them back to happiness and fullness of life."

As she finished the silent prayer that she had made for so many long months, Ann carefully set the screen in front of the fire. The movement of the screen and her clothing stirred a small flicker of flame to life among the blackened embers. Silhouetted by the tiny point of light, an unmistakable ship rode the red-hot waves—stout and proud.

Olive drab uniform of enlisted women; a winter uniform.

Tropical worsted uniform; a dress uniform for wear in summer.

WAC summer off duty dress for officers and enlisted women.

Coveralls; worn by many WAC's at work.

Official U. S. AAF photo

WAC in full field equipment.